STUFF H

"What happened, buddy?" Dad asks. "Did you and Kevin have a falling-out?"

That's his way of asking if me and Kevin had a fight, only Dad doesn't like to say the word.

"I dunno," I mumble. "Kevin's okay, as far as I know. I mean, it's not like I'm the boss of him," I try to explain, hoping this will get me off the hook. Because *no way* am I explaining to my dad what happened at school yesterday afternoon.

Me almost making Kevin cry. By accident.

"No-o-o," Dad says, a thoughtful look on his face. Well, he *always* has a thoughtful look on his face. That's because his brain is so gigantic, I guess.

"Maybe Kevin was sad about something else," I say.

Dad holds very still. "Something else?" he asks, his voice quiet. "Something other than what?"

Uh-oh, part two.

"Nothing," I say quickly. "You know school, Dad. Stuff happens there. You remember."

✳   ✳

BOOKS BY SALLY WARNER

* * *

THE ELLRAY JAKES SERIES

EllRay Jakes Is a Rock Star!

EllRay Jakes Is <u>Not</u> a Chicken!

EllRay Jakes Walks the Plank!

EllRay Jakes the Dragon Slayer!

EllRay Jakes and the Beanstalk

EllRay Jakes Is Magic!

EllRay Jakes Rocks the Holidays!

THE EMMA SERIES

Only Emma

Not-So-Weird Emma

Super Emma

Best Friend Emma

Excellent Emma

EllRay Jakes
Rocks the Holidays!

BY **Sally Warner**

ILLUSTRATED BY
Brian Biggs

PUFFIN BOOKS
An Imprint of Penguin Group (USA)

PUFFIN BOOKS
Published by the Penguin Group
Penguin Group (USA) LLC
375 Hudson Street
New York, New York 10014, U.S.A.

USA * Canada * UK * Ireland * Australia
New Zealand * India * South Africa * China

penguin.com
A Penguin Random House Company

Published simultaneously in the United States of America by Viking Children's Books
and Puffin Books, imprints of Penguin Young Readers Group, 2014

THE LIBRARY OF CONGRESS HAS CATALOGED THE VIKING EDITION AS FOLLOWS:
Warner, Sally, date-
EllRay Jakes Rocks the Holidays! / by Sally Warner ; illustrated by Brian Biggs.
Pages cm
ISBN 978-0-451-46909-0 (hardcover)
[1. Schools—Fiction. 2. Christmas—Fiction. 3. Family life—California—Fiction.
4. African Americans—Fiction. 5. California—Fiction.] I. Biggs, Brian, illustrator. II. Title.
PZ7.W24644Elj 2014 [Fic]—dc23 2013048390

Puffin Books ISBN 978-0-14-751251-2

Printed in the United States of America
Book design by Nancy Brennan

1 3 5 7 9 10 8 6 4 2

For my Canadian friends,

Nan and Wayne Cannon —S.W.

For Phyllis —B.B.

CONTENTS

* * *

✲ **1** ✲

RAINY SATURDAY

"This rain is wrecking my weekend," I tell Mom. I am staring out the kitchen window after a TV-and-cereal breakfast. We have all the lights on, it's so dark outside.

My dad and I usually do chores together on Saturday mornings. We eat a secret doughnut, too. But he's in sunny Arizona, looking at a meteorite. He's a rock scientist.

The way I learned it, it's called a *meteoroid* when it whizzes through space. That same space rock is a *meteor*—or shooting star—when it enters Earth's atmosphere and starts to burn up. And whatever is left is called a *meteorite* once it's on the ground.

You're welcome.

I memorized all that, and I *still* didn't get to go

to Arizona! My dad's giving a lecture at a university
in Phoenix on Monday, that's why.

"The rain's not wrecking your *whole* weekend," Mom reminds me, wiping her hands on the
clean kitchen towel she throws over her shoulder.
"Corey's spending the night with us, remember?
He'll be here at five. I'm making chili dogs."

"Oh, yeah," I say, smiling. Good old freckle-face
Corey Robinson! One of my two best friends in the
third grade at Oak Glen Primary School. And chili
dogs!

"I get to have *nobody*," Alfie says, kicking the leg of our kitchen table.

Alfie is my little sister. She's four. She is kind of a golden color. But she can cloud up fast, especially on a rainy Saturday in December.

"It's not fair," Alfie says, giving the kitchen table leg an extra-hard kick. "*Ow*," she cries, rubbing her small red sneaker.

"Santa's watching," I warn. "Don't forget, Alfie. He's making a list."

I am planning on using that sentence a lot this December, to keep Alfie from having too many meltdowns. They wear us out. Once we had to leave a movie before it even started, all because of Raisinets.

Alfie is against them.

"Santa is *not* making a list," Alfie says. "He doesn't even have a key to our house! Tell Santa not to make a list, Mom—or I'm calling 9-1-1. Because that's *spying*."

"You'd better *not* call 9-1-1, or you'll be in big trouble, young lady," Mom says, opening the freezer door. "You don't play around with that. Say. I have an idea," she says, her face hidden for a second by freezer mist. "How about if we make some of our famous oatmeal cookies for tonight? Corey loves them. And it'll be fun."

This is good news, because Mom's oatmeal cookies are *epic*. I brought a big batch to school once, and everyone loved them. Ms. Sanchez even took a bunch of them home in her plastic lunch container.

"I get to smash the eggs," Alfie says, her brown eyes sparkling. "Not EllWay."

That's how she says my name.

"You break eggs gently, you don't *smash* them," Mom says, putting some sticks of butter in the microwave to soften. "And we'll put them into a separate bowl first, this time," she adds.

Last time we made cookies, pieces of eggshell got into the cookie dough. That's what Mom's remembering.

My stomach is growling already!

"Mom?" I say, after the first two trays of cookies are in the oven, the timer's ticking, and a worn-out, cookie-dough-spattered Alfie is curled up on the family room sofa with her blankie, her thumb, and the newest *Fuzzy Kitties* DVD.

"Hmm?" she says, stirring milk into her coffee.

"Why did we move to Oak Glen?" I ask.

"Wait, what?" Mom says, surprised.

"Oak Glen," I repeat. "How come we moved here from San Diego?"

It happened when I was five years old. I wasn't exactly paying attention then.

To *anything*.

I couldn't ask this question if Dad was here, by the way. He'd prickle up and say, *"Why? What happened?"* See, there aren't too many families with brown skin in Oak Glen, and I sometimes get the feeling my dad is kind of ready for something to go wrong—even though nothing has. And I think he's the one who wanted us to move here.

"Why?" Mom asks. "What happened?"

I sigh. "Nothing *happened*," I say. "I was just wondering."

Rainy mornings do that to me.

But if Mom takes my rainy morning question in a bad way, she will probably call Dad on his cell.

And even if he were busy talking to an actual space alien who'd hitched a ride to Earth on that Arizona meteorite, he would take her call.

And then the uproar would begin—like it did a couple of months ago. That's when Alfie told Mom and me that she was feeling mad at Suzette Monahan, her friend-enemy at Kreative Learning and Playtime Day Care. And yes, we know they spelled "creative" wrong.

It turns out that Suzette was secretly charging other girls a penny to touch Alfie's hair, just because it's different from theirs.

WHOA. Get back!

Like Alfie was part of a petting zoo!

Alfie's moral of the story was that *she* should have gotten all those pennies. But I told her she had other reasons to be mad about what happened. I said that her hair was her own private property, and those girls should just keep their hands to themselves.

And to tell her teachers if it happened again.

But Mom told Dad, and Dad called the day-care ladies.

After four phone calls and one parents' meeting, the grownups decided to call the whole thing a misunderstanding. *"Everyone moved on,"* was the way Mom put it.

But I think my dad "moves on" slower than other people.

I just don't want the prickly-dad-uproar thing to happen again, that's all. You can't be a blend-in guy—my main goal in life!—if you're at the center of a tornado.

"Why did we move to Oak Glen," Mom says, repeating my original question. "Well, as you know, we were living in San Diego when you were little, honey," she says. "And we needed a bigger house after Miss Alfie came along."

"I know the living-in-San-Diego part," I say.

"So we were looking and looking for a new place, but it was a tough search," Mom continues. "You had just started kindergarten, EllRay. But one weekend, we decided to take a break and head up to Julian, to enjoy some of their apple pie."

Julian is a pretty mountain town with famous apples that is halfway between Oak Glen and Anza-

Borrego Desert State Park, a really cool area our family loves, especially Dad and me. It's our special place. Anza-Borrego has everything!

1. An oasis.
2. Bighorn sheep.
3. A badlands.
4. Mud caves.
5. Lots of earthquake faults, and you can even see where some of them split the rocks.

It's *awesome*.

"We stopped in Oak Glen on our way home," Mom says, remembering. "For gas, I think it was. And your dad really liked the way the place looked, so we popped into a real estate office before heading back down to San Diego."

I try to picture this, but it's hard to think of dad "popping into" any place. He's the type of guy who likes to think things through—mostly until you don't even feel like doing them anymore.

"I know, I know," Mom says, laughing as if she's just read my mind. "But you have to understand this about your father, EllRay. He can act on impulse when the spirit moves him. And once he realized how much bigger a house and yard we could afford in Oak Glen, and how good the schools were, he was sold."

"But what about you?" I ask, sneaking a look at my mom.

"I just wanted our search to be over, at that point," she says, still laughing. "I liked Oak Glen. And your dad promised he wouldn't mind the commute. He listens to audio books," she adds, sounding a little jealous.

"But you guys didn't know anyone here," I point out.

"We don't have family in San Diego anymore, either," Mom reminds me. "Of course, I missed my old hair salon so much that I finally decided to keep driving down to the city for my appointments. And I knew I'd miss my old Balboa Park writing group, but I have to admit that I've gotten a lot more actual work done since we moved. Fewer meetings, more writing."

"But didn't it bother Dad that there weren't that many brown faces walking down the street? I mean brown *legs*," I say, trying to correct myself.

Mom laughs. "As a matter of fact, we happened to *see* a number of brown faces that first day," she says. "Maybe that gave us a mistaken impression. We were both exhausted at that point, what with your dad's teaching and you two little rascals to take care of. He just threw himself into the house hunt, and *ta-da*! But we've all made good friends here," she adds. "And your dad feels that Oak Glen is becoming more diverse every year."

Not this year's third grade class at Oak Glen Primary School, I think, frowning.

But that's okay, because skin color isn't the reason I choose my friends.

"EllRay?" Mom is saying. "Everything is okay, isn't it, honey? I mean, you'd tell me if—"

"I'd tell you if," I say, nodding.

Before I'd tell my dad, I add silently.

"Everything's okay, Mom," I tell her as the oven timer dings and my stomach starts growling again. "Honest."

And it is. But *man*, I hope she doesn't mention this conversation to Dad.

✳ 2 ✳

BLENDING IN

"Pass me that brown crayon over there, okay?" I say to Corey, who is hunched over his white paper plate, dotting in a few of the three hundred freckles that cover his face. He swims every single day except Thanksgiving and Christmas, so he's outside all the time.

These round paper plates are for our self-portraits. A self-portrait is a picture you make that stars yourself, Ms. Sanchez says. It's like a selfie that you draw, Emma McGraw explained to Corey and me. She's a girl in our third grade class.

Corey is frowning, and his tongue is sticking out. He says drawing is hard, and his face shows it. He could swim a mile, easy, but sitting-down stuff knocks him out. "I want the *dark brown* crayon," I add, to make things easier for him.

It is Tuesday afternoon, and it's still raining. From big to little, all I can think of right now is Christmas, and next weekend, and my after-school oatmeal cookie snack, and finishing this goofy drawing of myself before the buzzer sounds so I don't have to work on it at home.

Our drawings are for the P.T.A. meeting. It is being held this Thursday night in the Media Center, which used to be called the library, someone said. Each month, a different class's artwork decorates the walls—in case the parents get bored, I guess.

This month comes our all-school holiday assembly. After that comes Christmas vacation, which we are supposed to call "Winter Break."

Today, our teacher, Ms. Sanchez, is standing in the corner of the room, laminating some old drawings and paintings for the Media Center walls, to go with our paper-plate faces. She must think the drawings and paintings look more important that way.

So we kids are basically on our own for a while.

"But you're not *dark* brown, EllRay," Fiona McNulty says, looking up from her own self-portrait.

"You should start with raw sienna. Then maybe use some burnt sienna, and a little chestnut for your cheeks, and *then* brown, but only for shading. Pass me the pink sherbet crayon, please, so I can do *my* cheeks."

Fiona is the best artist in our class. Maybe in any class at Oak Glen.

Or the world, for all I know.

She knows every color by name, like they are her own private pets.

"Ha ha," Jared Matthews cackles. "Burned sienna, EllRay. You're *burned*. Like toast, dude."

And his friend Stanley Washington pushes his glasses up on his nose, and he laughs, too. Most of the time, Stanley is like Jared's echo.

"Hey," Emma McGraw objects, and she stops drawing circles for her tangly hair. I can tell by her serious expression that she thinks Jared is making some crack about me having brown skin. She likes to stick up for the underdog, Ms. Sanchez said once, a couple of weeks after school started, and maybe Emma thinks she's doing that now.

For one crazy second, I thought "underdog"

meant a dog wearing underpants. That's why I remember it so well.

But having brown skin does not make me an underdog! And Jared's not talking about color, so Emma can just relax. Like, *forever*. When us guys say "burned," we mean insulted. And "toast" means that you're done.

Over.

DESTROYED.

Emma doesn't have to go turning it into some big deal.

Anyway, if it *were* a big deal, I could defend myself—even though like I said before, all I want in the whole wide world is to blend in.

And I keep getting singled out! I *hate* that.

"Burnt sienna is an official crayon color. They just spell 'burned' the old-fashioned art way," Fiona informs us, and like I said, she ought to know. She says she has all one-hundred-twenty official Crayola colors at home.

Fiona likes crayons better than markers, by the way. She says you can blend crayon colors together—the way she draws, anyway. Her blending-in skills are real feathery and gentle. Us boys mostly just lay the crayon colors on thick and fast, like there's a contest happening.

We like to get it over with.

Jared can't even use a crayon without making it snap in half!

Fiona says her favorite crayon color of all time is called inch worm, which is a green that our class doesn't have. We mostly have only the basic colors, and on top of that our crayons are kind of nubbly by now, not pointy the way they were last September.

But I guess nubbly, boring crayons are good enough for our paper-plate faces. Ms. Sanchez chose these plates, by the way, because they look like they have built-in frames where the outside circle part sticks out. I think we're going to glue red or green holiday glitter on the edges later. Glitter is Ms. Sanchez's best friend, she sometimes says.

She just means for art projects, though.

But it's true: glitter makes any goofy thing we make look like we did it on purpose. I'm not sure the Media Center lady will like getting glitter on her floor, though.

"Can I use the burnt sienna after you, EllRay?" Kevin McKinley asks. He is the only other boy in

Ms. Sanchez's class with brown skin. He's my other best friend, but not because of that. Well, not *only* because of that.

"You should start with sepia, Kevin," Fiona advises. "And then use brown, maybe with some salmon for your cheeks. Because your skin is darker than EllRay's. Only I don't know if we have sepia," she worries aloud. And she starts pawing through the crayons on our table for Kevin.

What's amazing is that Fiona is usually the shyest kid in our class. Art makes her brave, but only while we're doing it. Which isn't very often.

"Maybe I don't *want* salmon on my cheeks," Kevin mutters, scowling. "Mind your own business, Fiona," he adds, louder. And I don't blame him! Who is Fiona McNulty to go around saying what color a person's skin is?

Except I know she is speaking as an artist, not as a skin-color bossy person.

Still, I'm glad my dad is not here to hear this conversation. There would be a parents' meeting *for sure*.

"That's a rude thing to say, Kevin," Cynthia Har-

bison calls from the next table. She is like the girl version of Jared in our class. Lots of opinions, and all loud.

"Yeah," Heather Patton agrees. She is the girl version of Stanley, meaning that she is her hero Cynthia's loyal personal assistant. "You're practically saying Fiona should shut up, Kevin. And 'shut up' is against the law around here. It's a *swear*. Be careful, or we're telling!"

"Kevin never said 'shut up,'" Annie Pat Masterson says from the table next to ours, defending Kevin. "That was you, *Heather*."

Annie Pat is Emma McGraw's best friend, and she wears her bright-red hair in pigtails that stick out like warning cones. Her skin is so pale that she almost doesn't need to use any crayons at all when she colors in her face—although she'll probably use peach, which I heard used to be called "flesh color" in the olden days, until people looked around.

But some kids still say, "Pass the flesh, please," when they're coloring. Annie Pat's cheeks are pinker than usual. This happens when she gets mad.

Sometimes I get worn out from girls getting their feelings hurt.

It's hard to keep track of who is feeling what.

"I don't get why we even have to do this," Jared says, trying to color extra hair over his crayon ears, which he accidentally drew way too big.

Jared doesn't like being left out of any uproar.

"I guess it makes P.T.A. meetings more fun," Emma argues, maybe thinking it was a real question. "And parents like looking at art."

Emma doesn't like to stir up trouble, but she doesn't back away from it, either.

Even trouble with Jared.

"Huh. 'Parents,'" Cynthia says, shrugging. "Your dad's not even *here*, Emma. He lives in England. Remember? With his new family?"

I can hear Emma gasp, she's so surprised at Cynthia's fake-casual stealth attack—which breaks the number one kid rule about not talking about other kids' families.

Ever.

"Be quiet, Cynthia," Annie Pat says, defending her friend.

Worn. Out.

"P.T.A. meetings are dumb," Jared insists, glaring at Emma as if the whole open house thing was her bright idea. "My dad says so. That's why he never goes."

Me, I'm just glad we're not talking about skin color anymore—exactly the way Corey would be glad if we had been talking about freckles, and we stopped. Or the way Annie Pat would feel if we'd been talking about red hair.

I could go on and on with examples like that.

We're all basically happy with who we are, but I think no one wants too much attention.

It's not because there's anything wrong with brown skin that I'm glad the conversation has moved on. It's just that there aren't enough kids here at Oak Glen who *have* it.

That starts to make skin color a big deal, at least at times.

Not very often, though. And *PHEW!* for that.

✳ **3** ✳

HURT FEELINGS?

"Listen, everyone," Ms. Sanchez calls out two days later. "I've decided that this afternoon will be tidying time. I want your cubbies sorted, and the coat closet looking nice, even the lost-and-found box. Oh, and we need all your desktops spray-cleaned and sparkling. I have the supplies over by the sink."

It is Thursday, P.T.A. meeting day, and we just finished lunch. It started raining again toward the end, so some of the kids who were playing outside—like me and most of the boys—smell like wet sweaters and sweatshirts.

Well, like wet dogs, Cynthia said. And she has a dog, so she should know. A couple of the outside girls are fussing with their damp hair, which seems to have gotten either stringy or frizzy.

What is it with girls and their hair? I don't see

how they get anything else done in life. You should hear Alfie in the morning, when Mom's getting her three little braids ready for the day.

"Why?" Jared says, raising his hand a second later. "No one's gonna see our room, are they?"

"A parent or two might wander by after the meeting," Ms. Sanchez points out. "And we see it every day, don't we? Things around here have gotten pretty grubby, if you ask me. Now, let's all pair up so we can get to work."

Cynthia raises her hand. "I'll work with Heather,"

she says after Ms. Sanchez has called on her. "And I think Emma probably wants to work with Annie Pat," Cynthia continues, as if sorting people out is her job. "And Jared should work with Stanley, because they're the only ones who can stand each other."

"That's just fine," Ms. Sanchez says, sounding distracted as she heads for the sink. "Keep going, Miss Harbison," she adds over her shoulder.

"Okay," Cynthia calls out, looking important. "Well, EllRay should work with Kevin, of course," she says.

Wait, what? *Of course*? "But I want to work with Corey," I say, raising my hand—for Cynthia!—and talking at the same time.

See, Corey and I are still playing this game we invented last Saturday, when he spent the night at my house. It's a version of this really cool hand-held video game we both want for Christmas called *Die, Creature, Die*, only we made up our own story and words and rules. And we were taking turns telling each other more of the made-up story at lunch today. It would be fun to keep on doing it while we help clean the classroom. Since we have to clean the classroom, I mean.

"But Ms. Sanchez put me in charge," Cynthia says, like she's explaining something really obvious. "And you and Kevin *match*, EllRay. You go together."

We match.

She means we both have brown skin.

"Now, hold on a second," Ms. Sanchez says from across the room, actually raising both hands in a *stop-right-there!* kind of way. "No personal comments, if you please."

She doesn't just have eyes in the back of her head, she has ears there, too!

"I didn't say anything bad," Cynthia mumbles under her breath.

But Ms. Sanchez isn't letting this one slide. "Using your reasoning, Cynthia, perhaps I should put Corey and Annie Pat together, just because they both have freckles?" she pretend-asks.

And *that's* not a personal comment?

"Hey," Annie Pat murmurs, unexpectedly wounded.

WOW! Didn't she know she has freckles?

Annie Pat's cheeks turn pink under the cinnamon sprinkles scattered across her cheeks.

"Yeah," Emma chimes in. "And I thought Cynthia said Annie Pat was *my* partner. And EllRay wants Corey to be his partner. He just said so."

Kevin slides me a weird look. I can't crack the code of it.

Could he have hurt feelings?

But he's a boy!

It could just as easily have been *Kevin* who came over to spend the night last weekend, only he didn't. Or Kevin and I could have been the ones playing the made-up version of *Die, Creature, Die* at lunch today. Only we weren't. Kevin was busy playing Sky-high Foursquare with Jared, Stanley, and Jason Leffer, this other guy in our class. That doesn't mean we aren't still friends!

So me wanting to get paired up with Corey today is nothing personal against Kevin. It just happened that way.

Girls always seem sure about who they are friends with, by the way, but it changes a lot. In fact, they even rank their friends—like who is their first-best friend, their second-best friend, and so on. And the whole class knows every boring detail. *Always*.

With us guys, it's harder to tell who's friends or not. But basically, we're okay with most guys most days. And we all have a couple of friends we really *like* to hang with, like I do with Corey and Kevin.

The three of us are solid. I thought we were, anyway.

There might be some kid one of us is fighting with—but it is always finished in a flash.

Getting over hurt feelings moves faster for boys than for girls, in my opinion. Like water compared to mud.

"Your freckles are absolutely adorable, Annie Pat," Ms. Sanchez assures her. "I was merely trying to make a point, though I think it got lost somewhere along the way."

Cynthia whirls to face Kevin. "*Are* you friends with EllRay?" she asks, her hands on her hips. As if that's the point of this whole thing.

Kevin looks down at his sneakers. "I dunno. I thought so," he says, but his voice is so quiet that most kids can barely hear it.

I hear it, though. And it makes me feel really bad.

I clear my throat, wondering what I'm about to say.

"Shhh," Cynthia says, like I'm about to make everything worse—for *her*.

"Hah," Jared jeers. "Kevin got dumped! Even *EllRay* doesn't wanna hang with him."

Hey, wait a second. *"Even EllRay?"*

And I didn't dump anyone!

"They must have had a fight," Stanley says, jumping in. "Oh, EllRay," he coos, pretending to be Kevin. "Don't you *wuv* me anymore?"

"Be quiet," I tell him. "That never happened."

I try to catch Kevin's eye, but no go.

I know Kevin McKinley, though, and I can tell you this much for sure.

1. He doesn't care about us supposedly "matching."
2. Anyway, we don't match. He's a lot taller than I am.

3. And I don't think Kevin even cares who his partner is when he helps clean up. Big deal, right?

4. But I *do* know he doesn't like having this talk happen in front of everyone in class. That turned it *into* a big deal, which is embarrassing for him.

5. And Kevin *hates* being embarrassed—worse than anything.

In fact, he looks like he's about to start crying. And Kevin *never* cries.

How did this hurt feeling stuff happen? So fast, and out of nothing but spray bottles and cleaning rags?

I do not know what to do.

"This has gotten completely out of hand," Ms. Sanchez tells us, like we didn't already know. "But tick-tock, people. We are running out of cleanup time. Kevin, I'm going to ask you to be my special assistant for the afternoon, okay?"

Like that's supposed to make everything all better.

"Aww," Cynthia and Heather object at the same

time, because sometimes, being Ms. Sanchez's special assistant means that you get a Hershey's Kiss when you're done. And most girls are nuts for chocolate.

It's not science, Dad told me once, but it's true.

"'Aww,' nothing," Ms. Sanchez says, snapping out the words. "Each of you choose a partner *this minute*. And then each of you head over to the sink right now and grab a spray bottle or a cloth. And do a fabulous job."

"HUP! HUP!" Stanley Washington says, starting to march in place.

"Stanley," Ms. Sanchez says, warning him.

"But I meant that in a good way!" Stanley almost yelps.

And you can tell by his face that he's telling the truth.

"Get going, then," Ms. Sanchez says, laughing. "Start tidying!"

✳ 4 ✳

A FEW THINGS I'VE BEEN THINKING ABOUT

"Tell your mom I'm ready to go, buddy," Dad tells me on Thursday night, the car keys jingling in his hand. "I don't want to miss a minute of this meeting."

Okay. My dad is a big supporter of education, *obviously*, but I think he's being sarcastic. Having a nice relaxing night at home with the whole family is one of his rules. But tonight, he had to race back early from his college in San Diego and then "bolt down some food," as he put it, before it was time to leave for the six thirty P.T.A. meeting.

In other words, he wanted to stay home. But when you're talking parents and schools, here are a few things I've been thinking about. It's my longest list ever.

1. Parents are the bosses of kids, and they have lots of rules.
2. Schools are also the bosses of kids, and they have lots of rules, too. *Different* rules.
3. So us kids sometimes get stuck in the middle.
4. There are many school rules that parents cannot argue with—such as when school starts and finishes, stuff their kids are allowed to wear, and so on.
5. And there are a few squishier school things—not rules, exactly—that parents usually go along with, whether they deep-down want to or not. Attending P.T.A. meetings and parent-teacher conferences. Sending cans of food to school for food drives. Stuff like that.
6. So basically, when the parents' rules and the school's rules clash, like tonight, the parents usually go along with it for the sake of their kids.
7. But schools can also be a little nervous around parents, in my opinion. I think it's like schools never know what is going to set a prickly parent off: grades, skin color, religion, anything involving bringing money from home.

8. I think that's why schools usually make us kids be the ones to give the parents some kinds of news— about how we need to bring money for a field trip, or that there's going to be another parents' meeting, or that we have been exposed to lice or pinworms and the parents should do something about it. *Fast.*

Why have I been thinking about this so much? Because Alfie's hair-touching disaster last fall kind of freaked me out—with Dad suddenly questioning what was going on at Alfie's school.

If Kreative Learning and Playtime Day Care really counts as a school.

I don't want that kind of clash happening at Oak Glen Primary School. Life is hard enough, what with me being short, and eight, and accidentally hurting one of my best friend's feelings, which I didn't even think could happen, not with boys. The thought of my mom and dad being mad at Ms. Sanchez—or even Principal James—makes my stomach hurt.

I wouldn't want to have to choose who is right,

although I'm pretty sure my parents would get my vote—even if they were wrong.

We're like *family*.

Wait. I guess we are family!

"EllRay," Dad says. "Wake up. Please go tell your mother that the car is leaving in three minutes. Starting—*now*," he adds, tapping his watch.

GEEZ. Like her being late is all my fault! She's probably just trying to tell Melanie—our very cool teenage babysitter, who is in love with her cell phone and her boyfriend, in that order—what to do in case Alfie has a meltdown tonight.

Besides call her boyfriend.

But—"Okay," I say, and I scramble toward the sound of Alfie yelling about her pajamas not being cute enough to wear.

Not on such a special night as this.

I'm outnumbered, that's for sure!

✳ **5** ✳

THE OPPOSITE OF SKIN COLOR

"Hey, buddy. Got a minute?" Dad says the next night, Friday, coming into my room half an hour before bedtime.

"Sure," I tell him, already looking forward to his pretend-tough-guy knuckle-rub on my head, which is his version of a hug. I am on my bed, surrounded by a pile of the toy ads that were stuffed in this morning's newspaper. I've been making a holiday wish list and trying to find the perfect Christmas present for Alfie.

I'm thinking of getting my little sister a pink plastic pony with a silky dark mane and tail she can comb. She likes anything cute, and things she can comb, and this one pony I found even has great big green eyes. Perfect. It even has eyelashes.

"The worser the better," Mom jokes about Alfie's favorite toys.

Mom groaned at breakfast when she saw the Christmas ads. "Oh, not again," she said. "It seems like Christmas was *just last month*."

I don't get it! How can grownups feel that way? To me and all my friends, it seems as though last Christmas happened a hundred years ago!

And even if the grownups feel that way about it, they shouldn't say anything.

Why try to ruin it? Because Christmas is the *best*.

1. No school.
2. Presents.

3. Lots of parties and good stuff to eat. Chips and
    dips. Candy. And cookies.

What's so awful about that?

Dad piles up a few of the colorful ads to get
them out of the way, perches on the edge of my
bed, and reaches over to knuckle-rub my hair. "Are
you making a list and checking it twice?" he asks,
smiling as he looks at one of the ads.

"I think it's supposed to be Santa Claus who
does that," I tell him.

My dad sometimes gets the details wrong on
normal person stuff.

"So," Dad says, followed by—nothing.

Uh-oh. What's up? "We're still having Santa at
the assembly, aren't we?" I ask, because that's probably one of the things they talked about at the P.T.A.
meeting last night. And I look forward to those tiny
candy canes all year, because you can jam a whole
one in your mouth, and then you get a real drool-
factory going.

Only you have to remember to keep your mouth
shut, because—*slur-r-r-r-p!*

"It looks that way," Dad says, laughing. "A few members of the anti-sugar brigade didn't like the candy cane idea much, but I can't see Santa passing out celery stalks, can you?"

"Not really," I say, picturing the celery duels that would take place one second later. **WHACK! WHACK! WHACK!** "I guess Christmas and little candy canes just go together," I tell him.

"Not that they're going to be calling the assembly Christmas-*anything*," Dad says, sighing. "Principal James suggested 'A Holly Jolly Holiday' as one possibility of what to call it. He even mentioned 'Diversity Day.' But in the end, we decided to leave it up to you kids. The principal will be taking suggestions on Monday."

"Right. Us kids will come up with a name for the assembly," I tell him, angling my head for another knuckle-rub. "But let's stick with calling it Christmas here, okay? At least at our house."

"It's 'we kids,' buddy," Dad tells me. "And it's a deal. 'Christmas' it is. So. How's Kevin lately?" he asks, leaning back against a pillow. "His dad told me last night that he came home from school yesterday looking kind of down, only he wouldn't talk about it. But he seemed to think you might know why."

My heart goes **FLOOP**.Kevin was still acting a little weird today, I think, remembering. I thought he would have "come to his senses," as my mom sometimes says, and that his hurt feelings would have blown over by now.

"What happened, buddy?" Dad asks. "Did you and Kevin have a falling-out?"

That's his way of asking if me and Kevin had a fight, only Dad doesn't like to say the word.

"I dunno," I mumble. "Kevin's okay, as far as I know. I mean, it's not like I'm the boss of him," I try to explain, hoping this will get me off the hook. Because *no way* am I explaining to my dad what happened at school yesterday afternoon.

Me almost making Kevin cry. By accident.

"No-o-o," Dad says, a thoughtful look on his face. Well, he *always* has a thoughtful look on his face. That's because his brain is so gigantic, I guess.

"Maybe Kevin was sad about something else," I say.

Dad holds very still. "Something else?" he asks,

his voice quiet. "Something other than what?"

Uh-oh, part two.

"Nothing," I say quickly. "You know school, Dad. Stuff happens there. You remember."

"All right," Dad says. "Things happens at school. But you two have to stick together, EllRay—whether you want to or not."

Huh? "Why do we have to stick together?" I ask.

"You know why," Dad tells me.

"Because we both have brown skin?" I say, like I'm answering a test question.

Dad stares at a shark poster on the opposite wall.

"Me and Kevin are friends, Dad," I tell my father. "So you don't have to tell me to—"

"Kevin and I," Dad interrupts, still not looking at me.

"Kevin and I," I echo.

Dad's big on talking right. His latest thing is "Mister G." For example, if Alfie says, "I'm busy playin'!" instead of "playing," Dad will say, "What happened to Mr. G? Poor old Mr. G!"

To me, he's more likely to joke, "We paid for all

twenty-six letters in the alphabet, buddy. *Including* Mr. G, who lives at the end of many words. So let's put him there."

I know Dad's right, but it's hard to remember everything. And isn't what you say more important than how you say it?

Right now, I can't remember *anything*, I'm so nervous. Me and Dad—I mean *Dad and I*—hardly ever talk about skin color.

To tell the truth, I never used to think about what color I was when I was little.

And when my dad does *talk* about other people with brown skin, he usually says "the community." And by that, he does not mean Oak Glen.

"You don't even like Kevin's dad," I remind my father. "Not really. I heard you tell Mom once."

"You shouldn't eavesdrop, son," Dad says, giving me a look, and not the fun kind. "I like Kevin's dad just fine. I mean, we don't have a lot in common, but I like him."

"You have *something* in common," I say, keeping my voice quiet, to match his.

Dad finally smiles. "That's right, buddy. We're

linked. And that's what I'm talking about with you and Kevin. You're linked, too. And that link will seem more and more important to you as time passes. As you get older. Especially in a town like Oak Glen, where the community is so small."

Linked. Just like Cynthia Harbison said, Dad means that Kevin and I match—even though Kevin is taller than I am, and better at sports.

Also, Kevin's obviously a kid who gets his feelings hurt more easily than I do.

I think feelings are just *embarrassing.* The word "feelings" says it all, doesn't it? They're supposed to stay inside you, where they belong. Not get all blabbed about.

And our skin isn't even the same color brown!

But I guess people would say we *officially match.*

"Okay," I tell my dad. "But we don't have to think about that yet, Dad. Because *if* Kevin's mad at me, and I'm not saying he is, it doesn't have anything to do with skin color. It's the opposite, even."

"The opposite of skin color," Dad repeats, like it's almost a question.

That does sound kind of weird. I hope he doesn't ask me to "define my terms."

That's always scary with him.

"Well, I'll take your word for it, EllRay," Dad says, still smiling. "But I want you to promise to be open with me about what's going on at school."

"Okay, Dad," I say, crossing my fingers under the pink plastic pony ad.

I'll be a *little* open.

"Change of topic," Dad says, perching on the edge of my bed and reaching over to knuckle-rub my scalp. "What do you think about an after-Christmas getaway to Anza-Borrego, EllRay? Just you and I? No girls allowed. Anyway, they'll be off doing something special, too."

"Can we camp out?" I ask, my eyes wide.

He nods. "We *may*. Fingers crossed," he tells me. "If it's not too late to get a permit, and if the weather cooperates."

"Sounds good," I say, smiling big time. "Only I think I need a new sleeping bag. A mouse chewed up the corner of my old one," I remind him. "Remember? In the garage?"

"Darn mice," Dad says. "We'll keep your new bag in the house. How about that?"

"I'm getting a *new sleeping bag*?" I ask, eyes wide.

I hope it's a regular grownup one, not a skimpy bag with cartoon characters all over it. It gets cold in the desert at night!

"Well, Christmas is coming," Dad reminds me.

Which is completely unnecessary when you are talking to a kid about Christmas.

* 6 *

BRAINSTORM!

"There's EllRay," Jared and Stanley shout from across the playground on Monday morning, and they charge toward me like football players heading down the field. They're in the middle of some fantasy game, that's probably what's going on.

So I stand there and take it when they slam into me.

It's not like I'm gonna start *running* from them.

A bunch of girls swarm around us before things can develop any further. "Listen," Annie Pat Masterson says, her red hair shining in the sun. "My mom told me that the P.T.A. said each class is supposed to decide what they're gonna do for the assembly this Friday. We're supposed to brainstorm! That means everyone has to talk at the same time. So should we do a skit? With really cute costumes? I vote yes."

Annie Pat looks like she's ready to jump into a costume right now.

Stanley groans.

"Or singing?" Annie Pat's best friend Emma asks, ignoring the groan. "Only I don't know what we can sing *about*," she worries aloud. "Not if we have to take Christmas out of everything. That's what my mom told me the P.T.A. said we had to do, because of religion."

"We could sing 'Frosty the Snowman,'" Kry Rodriguez says, brushing her long bangs to one side. "I don't think snowmen are against anyone's religion."

"But a lot of the little kids at Oak Glen have never even *seen* snow," Emma points out. "So they'll just be more confused than they already are."

"Is Frosty the one who had a very shiny nose?" Fiona McNulty asks. She's the crayon artist, remember? She says she has weak ankles, even though she walks just fine. So I don't know.

"I think that was Rudolph," Kry says. And she's usually right about things.

"I thought we were just supposed to figure out what to call the *assembly*," I say. "That's what my dad told *me*. But maybe we should leave the word 'snow' out of the assembly title, too, like with 'Christmas,' since it never snows in Oak Glen, California."

"It did once, I think," Kry says, tapping her chin and looking up at the sky through her bangs as if the answer might be written on today's puffy white clouds. "In the olden days."

"Dang! And we missed it," Corey says, kicking some leaves that look like little gold inside-out umbrellas.

"Hey," I say, giving him a friendly shove. "When did you get here?"

I look around for Kevin, but he's not on the playground yet.

"There's a real good song called 'Walking in a Winter Wonderland,'" Emma says, like she's thinking aloud. "So maybe we should call the assembly that. Because you can have a 'winter wonderland' without any snow."

"How?" Jared asks, his hands on his hips. "The *whole entire song* is about how much fun it is knocking down some dude's snowman. So *duh*."

Okay, two things. First, it's like we are brainstorming without a brain, me included. And second, I'm pretty sure that's not the only thing the song 'Walking in a Winter Wonderland' is about, but it's too early in the day to argue.

Especially with Jared.

It's like Jared eats arguments for *breakfast*, he loves them so much. Arguments give him energy, like a vampire slurping up blood.

Not that that's a very Christmassy comparison to make.

But in fact, even when everyone is happy and things are going great, Jared sometimes likes to get mad in advance.

Just in case!

"I like that idea," Kry says thoughtfully, her dark brown eyes shining. "Because 'winter wonderland' can also mean sparkly decorations and fun. Without the snow. So that would be a good thing to call the assembly. We just won't sing the song," she adds, probably to make Jared feel better.

"If you say so," he mumbles.

Kry's about the only kid Jared won't take on. I think he kind of likes her.

"She just *did* say so," Emma tells him, fake-innocent.

"So, we'll tell Ms. Sanchez that 'Winter Wonderland' is our suggestion for the assembly title," Cynthia says, like she's been taking notes. "But what song are we gonna sing?"

"We'd better figure something out," Heather says, sounding gloomy. "Or they're gonna make us sing 'Jingle Bells' again, like last year. While we **JANGLE** those old *bells*."

"And while the boys sing all the wrong words," Cynthia says, shaking her head in disgust.

I forget the wrong words, except for "Batman smells."

Maybe this won't be so bad after all!

"Let's do that one again," Stanley says, laughing.

This reminds me to look around for Kevin again. Is he here yet?

Sort of. He has appeared out of nowhere and is sitting on the boy's lunch table, pawing through his lunch sack, even though school hasn't started yet.

Us guys do that. That's why we're always starving by the time we get home from school.

Kevin is continuing to ignore me—because I embarrassed him in public last Thursday. Accidentally, but what difference does that make?

I don't blame him for being mad, now that I think about it. Someone can *accidentally* knock you over during recess, can't they? And it can hurt just as much as if they aimed themselves at you with a giant slingshot.

"C'mon," Emma says through a tangle of wind-blown curly hair. "We have to come up with something *good* to sing this year. We don't want to just stand there shaking a bunch of rusty old bells. That's so babyish."

"Yeah," Annie Pat says, seconding her. "And the assembly is this Friday, in only four more days. And we want to look good, *whatever* we do."

"We should dance," Kry says, inspired.

Yeah. *That's* gonna happen.

Jared makes a few hurling sounds, and Stanley pretend-dances to them.

"The girls, anyway," Emma says, seeing the expression on my face. "But what kind of dance?"

"I've got an idea," Cynthia says, and Heather gets ready to back her up no matter what. You can see it happen. "My mom listens to this old song called 'Jingle Bell Rock,'" Cynthia tells us, "and it's really cute. We can tell Ms. Sanchez we want to do that one—before she sticks us with 'Jingle Bells' again."

"I think I know that song," Kry says, beaming at her. "And it's *adorable.* Good one, Cynthia."

"Thanks," Cynthia says, looking surprised and bashful at the same time.

Everyone likes Kry. I don't know how she does that!

"I don't wanna do *anything* 'adorable,'" Corey mutters in my ear. And I kind of agree.

But I don't have any better ideas, and the buzzer just sounded.

I feel myself being pulled along with the crowd of kids as we make our way toward the school building.

"Dude," a voice behind me shouts, cutting through the noise around us.

Kevin.

"Hey," I say over my shoulder. I attempt a smile. "Listen, Kev. I'm really—"

"I decided you owe me, EllRay," Kevin says. "*Big-time.*"

"What are you talking about?" I ask.

"I'm talkin' about makin' things even," he says.

Talkin' and *makin'*?

But I decide not to say anything to Kevin about 'poor Mr. G,' to use Dad's expression. Not that I would.

"I'll tell you the rest later," Kevin adds as we push our way past the heavy door to Ms. Sanchez's third grade class. "After I figure it out."

He'll tell me the rest later.

Lucky me.

But at least Kevin's talking to me again!

* 7 *

DOWN THE RABBIT HOLE

"You boys go straight to Principal James's office, give him this, then come right back," Ms. Sanchez tells Kevin and me an hour later at her classroom door. She hands me an envelope that I guess is full of our brainstorm ideas for the assembly title and the song we would not refuse to sing, "Jingle Bell Rock."

"That's okay. EllRay can go alone," Kevin tells her.

"That's okay," she echoes, smiling. "But no, he can't. You're going together. And *now* would be good."

"She didn't lick it shut," Kevin tells me as we head off down the empty hall.

Down the rabbit hole.

I started calling it "going down the rabbit hole" last year, the few times I was allowed out into the empty hall during class hours, usually to deliver a message to the office or to use the restroom. Mom was reading Alfie and me *Alice's Adventures in Wonderland* at the time, which is definitely not just a girl book, by the way. I think I got the words "hole" and "hall" mixed up.

But being alone in an empty school hall seemed strange to me back then, like Alice falling down the rabbit hole. That's my point. One minute, normal. Next minute, weird.

The hall seems weird today, too, even though I'm with Kevin. It's like I can still hear the ghosts of sneakers squeaking and kids shouting, even though there's nobody here except Kevin and me—and about a hundred brightly colored construction paper snowflakes pinned to the wall.

A few of them are fluttering for no reason, which is *also* weird. And a little scary.

Emma McGraw was right. Those fake snowflakes—and the smallest one is the size of a Frisbee—are the closest lots of kids here in Oak Glen, California, have ever been to snow. So far, anyway. They've probably seen real snow in movies, but maybe even *that* wasn't real. Maybe—

"I *said*, Ms. Sanchez didn't lick the envelope shut," Kevin repeats, interrupting my thoughts. "So we could look inside."

"We'd better not," I tell him. "We already know what's in it, don't we? And there are probably security cameras all around us."

This seems to impress Kevin. "*Dude*," he whispers, darting nervous glances at the red fire alarm boxes on the walls and the emergency sprinklers on the ceiling. The sprinklers here at Oak Glen Primary School look like little upside-down space capsules. They could *definitely* be hiding security cameras inside.

"So, listen," Kevin whispers, giving up on us snooping inside the envelope. "Like I said before school, you *owe* me. You know, for throwing shade last week."

"Throwing shade?" I repeat.

I have heard this expression before. I just can't remember what it means.

"You know," Kevin says, shaking his head as we

pause near a "What Not to Bring to School" poster. "Pretending to give a kid a compliment, when you're really dissing them. Like, 'Oh, you're so brave going out in public with that haircut!'"

Oh. Okay.

Kevin has a teenage sister who thinks she's the expert on everything. Tania, I think her name is. She's big into hip-hop, and most other kinds of dance, too.

And she talks like she's on a reality TV show. "Throwing shade" must be coming from her.

"But I didn't—"

"*Pretending* in front of everyone that you really wanted to clean desks with me?" Kevin interrupts, like he's making this really obvious point. "Because we're such good friends? Only you already had all these plans with Corey? You made me look bad in front of everyone—*on purpose*. You disrespected me, dog. I looked like a fool."

This sounds like pure Tania to me. She got him all worked up.

We are deep into "The Land of Hurt Feelings," as Mom calls it when she's talking about Alfie and her friends at Kreative Learning and Playtime Day Care. And hurt feelings mean Girl Land. In my opinion, anyway.

Not that I'm telling Kevin that.

"So, you'll have to do whatever I say, so we can be even," he tells me.

"What are you talking about?" I ask. "Can't you just sock me one, and get it over with?"

"You embarrassed *me*," Kevin says, ignoring what I just said as he spells it out. "So I get to embarrass *you*. That'll make us *even*, and then we can be *friends* again. I figured it all out."

He sounds so sure of himself! And he's always been obsessed with things coming out even. Potato chips. Cookies. Taking turns playing a game. The number of pillows he has during a sleepover.

"But I'm *already* embarrassed," I try to explain. "Especially lately. Just walking around, even. I stick out like a sore thumb! Can't I just tell you I'm sorry?" I ask. "Or—how about if I apologize in front of everyone at lunch? That would make me suffer."

"Not enough," Kevin says. "Anyway, that would only make you look better and me look worse, Ell-

Ray. And you know it! No, you gotta do a challenge. At *least* one. And I get to say what it is."

"A **CHALLENGE**?" I say, echoing his words. "Is that like a dare? Because we're not allowed to do dares. Remember? It's against official Oak Glen Primary School rules."

"A challenge is different from a dare," Kevin says.

"I guess you're right," I say, thinking about it. Because you can challenge yourself, can't you? To do better at something: a spelling test, jumping far, raising your score in a game. Or you can challenge a friend to do something as well as you can, like in a contest, or to do better at something than he did before. But throwing down a dare is trying to make someone do something he does not want to do.

"Of course I'm right," Kevin says, looking prissy as he lifts his chin in the air.

His *brown* chin.

"Listen," I tell him, inspired. "We gotta stick together, Kev—because of the *community*. Because we're *linked*."

I don't really see it, not the way Dad means. At least not yet.

But hey. Anything's worth a try.

"What are you talking about?" he says, looking madder than before, even.

"I *mean*, we both have brown skin," I inform him—as if he didn't already know.

"Oh, that," Kevin says, shrugging. "I thought you were talking about us being friends."

"We're linked that way too," I say, nodding.

"Well, we're not linked like *anything* until you do my challenges," Kevin announces. "You must successfully complete them," he adds, as if he has just been given magical wizard powers.

And did you notice? Now, it's definitely more than one challenge!

"Whatever, dog," I tell him, a hopeless feeling settling over me like a pile of too-heavy blankets on a hot night. "Just tell me what I have to do."

"I'm not done thinking them up yet," he says, chin still high in the air. "But I'll let you know when I do. Now, let's go, before Ms. Sanchez starts looking for us."

And even though I'm the one holding the envelope, Kevin leads the way down the empty hall to Principal James's office. And here's me trotting along behind him, deeper down the rabbit hole.

Man, I think, struggling to keep my legs going.

This is going to be *one bad week*.

✳ 8 ✳

PRINCIPAL HAIRY JAMES

"Well, well, well. If it isn't EllRay Jakes and the Kevinator," Principal James says as we slink into his holiday-decorated office. "I've been wondering where you two were. I was about to send out a search party," he adds, glancing at his watch.

Yes, he still wears a watch instead of just looking at his cell. So does my dad.

I think Principal James is joking about the search party. But if there was one, I can imagine what the flyers he would hand out might say.

LOST!

THE ONLY TWO BOYS WITH BROWN SKIN IN MS. SANCHEZ'S THIRD GRADE CLASS!

"I'm sorry we're late," I tell him. "It was—the hall."

"Yeah. Sorry. The hall," Kevin—the Kevinator?—echoes.

"The other class representatives have come and gone," Principal James says, ignoring our lame excuse. "May I have the envelope, please?"

I hand it over, knowing what's inside.

Principal James reads the two pieces of paper that were inside the envelope as Kevin and I edge toward the door, hoping to make our getaway. But no such luck.

"Have a seat, boys," he tells us, still reading. "Hmm. I like both these ideas. I'll give Ms. Sanchez a jingle so she doesn't worry, because I'd like you to stick around for a moment," he adds, reaching for the phone on his desk.

Cool! *Maybe*.

Principal Harry James—which I secretly spell Principal *Hairy* James, because of the beard on his face—is okay for such a big, scary guy.

Well, he's only scary because you have to go to his office for a talking-to if you get in trouble.

But most of the time, he's nice. He stands on the school's front steps every morning, greeting each of us by name. I think he must study flash cards at home. And he's there when school lets out, too, to say good-bye. Alfie calls him the "hello and good-bye man."

She'll learn how important he is soon enough. Next year, in fact.

Watch out, Oak Glen Primary School!

The principal murmurs into the phone for a few seconds, then perches his skinny rear end on his desk and faces Kevin and me.

"Relax," he says, smiling through his beard as he rearranges a couple of the snow globes on his desk. "You're not in any trouble, guys. But you came all this way down that *hall*," he says, fake-shuddering.

Wait. Is he making fun of my lame excuse for being late to his office?

"So, you might as well stay so we can talk about Friday's assembly," he continues. "Because planning it this year has been a real headache, let me tell you. But your class has saved the day. We'll call it *An Oak Glen Winter Wonderland*, just to make it our own. That has a real ring to it, don't you think?"

He isn't worried by the fact that there isn't anything very Winter Wonderland-y at all about Oak Glen in the winter. Sometimes the weather pours down rain and wrecks people's outside decorations. Sometimes there's a Santa Ana windstorm, and pitiful dried-up old Christmas trees roll around in the gutters, making Alfie want to adopt them and take them home, even though Christmas is over. Sometimes it gets strangely cold, and plants keel over and die.

That's about it.

FA LA LA LA LA.

"I was thinking of dividing the morning up into two assemblies," Principal James tells us. "That way, we'll have enough room in the back of the auditorium for your families to be comfortably seated. So the first assembly will be kindergarten through third grade, and the second will be fourth through sixth grades. Good idea, right?"

Kevin gives me a blank look.

"Sure," I tell the principal. "And each assembly will be shorter, too. So that makes it a *great* idea."

"And here's where you two come into the picture," Principal James says, springing it on us. "Since the third graders will be top dogs in the first assembly, I thought I'd ask one of you two boys to be the emcee."

"What's an emcee?" Kevin asks, sounding suspicious.

"It stands for M. C., 'Master of Ceremonies,'" Principal James tells us. "That means you welcome everyone to the show, introduce each act, then say good-bye at the end of our Winter Wonderland assembly."

"Kevin would be *great* at that," I say, hoping that this act of generosity will convince Kevin that we're friends again.

Not to mention that being emcee of anything is the last thing I'd ever want to do.

Being an emcee is almost the *definition* of sticking out. Of not blending in.

So, "win-win," as my dad sometimes says.

"Yeah, I *would* be great," Kevin agrees. "Only I think EllRay should do it."

What?

"And he really wants to do it, too," Kevin continues, sliding me an evil grin. "Don't you, EllRay?"

"I—I—"

"*Don't* you?" Kevin asks again, giving me another look.

A look that says, *This is one of your challenges, dude. And you have to do it.*

"I guess so," I tell Principal Hairy James. "I mean, sure. I'll do it."

"And you'll do a terrific job, too, EllRay," our

principal informs me, unaware of the fainting, the hurling, or the other body calamities that might happen once I'm up there on the stage.

HO, HO, HO.

"So, good," Principal James says. "*That's* settled. Now, I think it's about time for you two boys to get back to class, don't you? And watch out for that *hall*," he pretend-warns.

"We will," Kevin and I say together, though I barely manage to peep out the words.

"Great. Then off you go," Principal James says, shooing us out through his silver garland-hung doorway.

And I don't look at Kevin the whole way back to Ms. Sanchez's room.

I'm *that mad*.

9

HANGING OUT IN THE KITCHEN

"Did you finish your homework?" Mom asks after dinner on Tuesday night.

"Mm-hmm," I say.

She and I are hanging out in the kitchen, scarfing down the leftover crispy pieces of cheese that overflowed and melted in the pan. We had grilled cheese sandwiches for dinner tonight, and about three veggies, as usual.

Carrot sticks, lettuce salad, and something Mom calls "three-bean salad."

Alfie said "No way!" to that last one. But I ate all three beans. One each.

Dad's at some meeting at his college in San Diego. That's why we didn't have meat for dinner tonight. See, Dad—and I!—love meat, but Mom likes to make anything that's *not* meat, when he's not home.

Alfie loves chocolate and buttered noodles, mostly.

She's playing in her room. I can hear her talking to her dolls from here.

"How about the lyrics to your assembly song?" Mom asks over her shoulder as she loads the dishwasher. "Have you memorized those?"

"Not all of them. Not yet," I say, trying not to sound too relieved.

Ms. Sanchez loved the idea of "Jingle Bell Rock." She even said okay to the dancing. So, because of the **JINGLING** feet mentioned in the song, which don't even make sense, the girls plan to wear bells strapped around their ankles—and just dance like crazy. Someone's mom is sending away for new bells. She even paid extra for super-fast delivery, so they'll get here on time.

With any luck, no one will be able to hear us sing.

But the girls are so excited now about getting to dance onstage that I don't think they're even bothering to learn the words—so us boys better know them.

It is going to be a *disaster*, because . . .

1. Jared uses the same musical note for every word he sings. He sounds like someone using a buzz saw.
2. Corey has decided to just move his lips and pretend to sing.
3. Stanley sings really loud, but he never gets the words right.
4. And so on.

But at least we'll be the oldest kids there, so no big kids can laugh at us.

"Why don't you sing me the song right now?" Mom suggests, smiling. "At least try."

"No, thanks," I mumble. Performing it once on stage—in front of moms, dads, and video cameras—will be bad enough. I just hope we don't end up on YouTube.

And I also have to be the emcee!

This is like a nightmare come true for me. Everyone will be *staring*.

"Well then, why don't you go see what your little sister is up to?" Mom says. This sounds like more of a question than it is.

"Alfie seems to be arguing with someone," Mom adds, smiling.

"Probably one of her dolls," I say.

Alfie has a very active imagination.

And she has tons of dolls.

"You go settle things for them," Mom tells me, smiling. "You know Alfie. Sometimes she needs a little help sorting things out. And who better for that than her big brother?"

"Okay," I say, hiding my sigh as I pry up one last bit of cheese before I go.

See, spending time with Alfie can make a person dizzy. She's like Jared, a *little*, because she likes to argue just for the fun of it. And she always thinks she's right—even though she's only four!

Also, Alfie can chatter about a five-minute *Fuzzy Kitties* cartoon for fifteen minutes, easy. It makes my brain hurt.

"Go on," Mom urges. "Tell her it's almost time for her bath, okay? Ten minutes."

Alfie needs lots of advance notice—about doing anything.

Ten-minute warnings. Five-minute warnings. One-minute warnings. It's like she's a space shuttle always about to blast off.

My dad says Alfie "has trouble with transitions," whatever that means.

It sounds like he's saying that my little sister doesn't know how to fix car engines, but I know that can't be right.

"Scoot," Mom says.

But I don't just scoot, I skedaddle.

✳ 10 ✳

OFFICIALLY BROWN

"Knock, knock," I say, pausing outside Alfie's room. Her door is open, but I'm trying to teach her not to barge into *my* room without knocking. See, I'm setting an example.

So far, so bad.

Alfie looks up from a row of six or seven Barbies lying on her fluffy carpet. Three of them have Beyoncé-brown skin. They are all wearing fancy dresses. Their feet are all touching a yardstick, which is a long ruler that I guess Alfie is pretending is the ground. "Is this gonna be a knock-knock joke?" she asks, getting ready to not laugh.

"Nope," I tell her. "I'm supposed to tell you that you have to take a bath in ten minutes. So, ten-minute warning. What are you doing?" I say, already half sorry I asked, because her explanation might be a real brain-frazzler.

"We're having a beauty contest," she informs me. "First prize is a brand-new darling outfit. Right now they're telling their hobbies," she adds. "This one likes horseback widing," she says, pointing.

That's Alfie-speak for "riding."

"And this one likes shopping," she continues. "Actually, all of them like shopping."

I go closer to take a look. "Who's winning so far?" I ask, plopping down next to her.

"She is," Alfie says, pointing to her newest doll, one with long, blonde hair. "Because her hobby is collecting stuffed animals. I wish they made little stuffed animals for Barbies," she adds, forgetting about the contest for a minute. "I'd buy a whole lot of them! *Tons.*"

"I know you would," I say, picturing it. "But what about this doll?" I ask, pointing at one of the brown-skinned dolls. "She's pretty, isn't she?"

Because—Alfie's pretty, too. And *she* has brown skin.

"Yeah," Alfie says. "Vanessa. But she's stuck-up and mean. Like Suzette Monahan," she explains, naming her secret enemy—sometimes, anyway— at Kreative Learning and Playtime Day Care. "Mom and Dad were talking about you yesterday, EllWay," she says, jumping to another subject like she always does.

"You were listening in?" I ask, frowning.

"Not on purpose," Alfie says. "I was hiding under the dining table, behind the tablecloth. Pwetending to be a mouse. And they just started talking."

"Huh," I say, wondering what they might have said. A "Needs improvement!" comment on a progress report can really set them off, especially my dad. So can any remark by Ms. Sanchez having to do with my so-called organization skills.

Who even *wants* to be organized? I think keeping things organized is boring—and *hard*. When I pull my notebook out of my backpack when I get home, I never know what's gonna fly out and hit the ground. Old permission slips, party invitations, stuff I found on the sidewalk on the way home, sandwich halves I was saving for later. It's kind of exciting!

But that's why Mom has started sitting down with me on Sunday nights, so we can go through my backpack—and notebook—together.

I think that's treating me like a baby. But my mom says it's important.

"They were talking about you being king of the school assembly," Alfie whispers, as if the blabber-mouth Barbies might spread this stupendous news all around.

"I'm not *king*," I tell her. "I'm just the emcee. That's like an announcer," I add, before she can ask. "And the assembly is only for kids up to the third grade. And I only got named emcee because Ms. Sanchez told me to go to the principal's office in the first place. And because the principal wanted to get the assembly planning over with, once and for all. And because Kevin wouldn't do it. That's *why*. It's not like kids voted for me."

"Mom told Dad it was because you were a born leader," Alfie informs me.

A born leader.

Yeah, right!

I can lead the way when it comes to not getting permission slips signed, I guess. And I'm a born leader at losing socks. And I am the leader at hurting one of my best friend's feelings without really knowing how it happened.

I can even lead the way down the rabbit hole to the principal's office.

What I *can't* lead the way at is being someone who does not **STICK OUT**.

And that would be so much more *relaxing* in life, not to have to worry all the time about people noticing me. Especially for the wrong reasons!

And I'm not saying that just because I am one of not-too-many kids with brown skin at a school with mostly white kids, either. Well, sort of *pink* kids, to tell the truth. Or freckled, or sometimes even a little tan.

But that's not the same thing as being officially brown.

And it's not like I wouldn't stick out anyway, even if my skin was pink, too. I'm the shortest kid in the whole third grade. And face it, I have a weird name.

The brown skin part just makes it a triple-header. It's like the cherry on the sundae.

"And then Dad said he was pwoud of you," Alfie says, thinking it over.

Proud of me? For accidentally being named the emcee?

Listen. There's tons of good stuff I've done that he doesn't even know about!

1. I was nice a few times to this goofy kid in second grade who everyone was making fun of for dragging his blankie to school. In fact, I told them to cut it out.
2. And once, I secretly gave Annie Pat my sweatshirt to wear when she got the extreme shivers on the playground.
3. But I didn't make any lame excuses to my mom when Annie Pat forgot to give it back. I just took the heat.
4. And I watch Alfie's back all the time.

But Dad's proud of *this*? Me being named the emcee—almost by accident?

"He's pwoud of me, too," Alfie hurries to tell me. "All the time, not just on assembly day. And I'm coming to your Winter Wonderland show, by the way," she adds, bouncing on to yet another topic.

"I don't think so," I say carefully. "You'll probably be busy having too much fun over at Kreative Learning and—"

"I'm *coming*," she informs me. "You may be the king of the show, EllWay. But I get to be the king's sister."

"Okay, good," I say, scrambling to my feet. "That's just fine. See you there, Alf. And it's your bath time, by the way."

"But you didn't give me the five-minute warning," Alfie tells me, shaking her head. "*Or* the one-minute warning." And she busily switches a couple of Barbies around—so that the stuck-up, mean one is at the very end of the line.

Take *that*, Vanessa-Suzette.

"I'll let Mom give you those two warnings," I

say, feeling fed up and sad at the same time.

Because—Dad probably thinks that me being an emcee at the assembly will be good for the *community*. For everyone with brown skin. I just figured that out. And it makes me feel terrible! I can't live up to that. I'm just an ordinary kid, with good parts and bad parts all scrambled together.

What if I accidentally mess up, like I did with Kevin's friendship?

And what about what's good for *me*?

* 11 *

CHALLENGE

"Hey, EllRay-dude," Kevin says, coming up to me after lunch.

It is Wednesday, December seventeenth, and most of us ate outside—even though it is kind of cold, and the wind is blowing leaves and escaped sandwich bags around in circles, and puffy clouds are whizzing across the sky.

It's actually great playing weather, though. We should get to stay outside the whole rest of the day, just flinging ourselves around. Most of us boys are allergic to sitting still, except when we're playing video games.

And guys crashing into each other can be *awesome*.

"What, Kevin-dude?" I say, trying for a regular smile.

But I have been dreading this moment. What goofy thing is he going to come up with next for me to do?

"I got one," Kevin tells me. "Your first challenge." And a small crowd of guys quickly gathers around, as if they can somehow tell that something unusual—maybe even interesting!—is about to make their lunch break more lively.

Jared. Stanley. Even a worried-looking Corey.

"Wait. *Wait*," I say. "I already agreed to be the emcee for the assembly. I thought that was my first challenge. How many are there gonna be? You can't keep adding on," I say, trying to act like I have a choice about doing them.

Which I don't. Not if I want to make it up to Kevin so we can be friends again.

I really do owe him, even though it was an accident that I embarrassed him.

And with Kevin, once we're even, it'll be over.

Done with.

Forgotten.

Gone.

He's cool that way.

"Three challenges, *not counting* being the emcee," Kevin announces. "Because in books, everything happens in threes, doesn't it? Three wishes. The three wise men."

"But I think the wise men were from the Christmas story," I say cautiously, not wanting to set him off again.

"Well, *that's* in a book," Kevin says.

No arguing with him there. "Okay," I tell him in my most soothing voice. "What do I have to do?"

"Hang from the middle of the overhead ladder for a real long time," Kevin says. "Until the buzzer sounds. Starting—*now*."

And I try to hide my smile as our windblown posse heads toward the overhead ladder. Kevin's first challenge will be an easy one for me! I'm really good at overhead ladder stuff.

I mean, I've never tried just hanging from it, but it *sounds* easy.

Oak Glen Primary School's overhead ladder is metal, and it's tall. There's sand underneath. A couple of rungs on each side serve as steps. You climb up and then reach over to grab on to one of the top rungs. Then you swing hand over hand across all the top rungs of the structure until you get to the other side.

It's more fun than it sounds, which is true of most things us kids like to do.

But Kevin doesn't want me to swing my way *across* the overhead ladder. He wants me to swing my way to the middle and then stay there, holding on like crazy. The only problem will be that other kids—mostly first- and second-graders—are already using it. So I get in the line and wait my turn to swing to the middle and hold on, no matter what.

Okay. *It's my turn.*

And—I'm up the side rungs.

I grab hold of the first top rung—it's cold!—and start swinging toward the middle rung. I can almost taste the cold metal in my mouth, which is weird.

Swinging, swinging, swinging, swinging, *STOP*.

And—I'm hanging, holding on with my too-small, puny hands.

Little hamster paws, they feel like.

And that's when the "hold on, no matter what" part turns out to be harder than I thought. Because once I'm hanging there, the little kids keep trying to swarm past me.

They don't get it yet, that this is a big-deal, third grade challenge!

1. One chunky first-grader with red hair comes chugging past like I'm invisible, his legs flailing as he kicks my shins. Not on purpose, but it still hurts.

2. Two tiny girls swing right by me, one on either side, chattering the whole way. They couldn't stop talking for a minute, even? Why do girls talk so much? At least it's not just Alfie who does it! I was starting to think there was something wrong with her.

3. A feisty second-grader with a mean glint in his eye swings his way toward me from the wrong direction, and then tries to go through me, basically. "Move it! Move it!" he keeps yelling as he kicks at me, even though I'm older than he is. "You're hogging the whole thing! No fairsies!"

Meanwhile, down on the sand, Kevin, Corey, Jared, and Stanley are watching me. Corey looks like he's counting under his breath. His lips are moving. And then up come Emma, Annie Pat, and Kry.

Oh, great, I think, as my hands start to sweat and burn at the same time, and as my head starts to feel like a water balloon about to explode.

Witnesses.

✳ **12** ✳

TICKLISH?

A-million-and-one.

A-million-and-two.

A-million-and three.

That's what it seems like, anyway.

At least I don't have to use the restroom!

And the second I think that, I *do* need to use the restroom. Why does that always happen?

Think of something else, I order myself. *Anything* else. Think about the broiling hot Anza-Borrego desert in the summer, or Christmas morning, or decorating cookies with a whole bottle of sprinkles—and then eating them. Think about being a superhero in the game of *Die, Creature, Die*, and about staying up late, and *no school*.

Do not think about having to use the restroom.

Do not think of how much your hands hurt.

I already have calluses, sure. But they're tiny, the size of Alfie's fingernail clippings.

My arms feel hot and heavy, and my feet are numb. I'd kick them, just to get them back to normal, but then I'd fall to the ground for sure.

And so I just hang there.

A-million-and-twenty.

A-million-and-twenty-one.

Jared's getting bored, I can tell. And then he gets this look on his face. "I wonder if EllRay's ticklish?" he asks no one in particular.

But he asks it *loud.*

And he shoves to the front of the little-kid-line, climbs up a rung, then grabs on to an overhead rung with both gigantic hands. He swings my way. "Here I come, EllRay," he calls out. "Are you ticklish, dog? *TICKA, TICKA, TICKA*! And you'd better hang on, or your stupid, show-off trick—whatever it is—won't count. And you'll have to start *all over.*"

Start all over? No way! But I'm too worn out to argue.

Now Jared is hanging at my side. I can smell bologna on his breath.

He lets go of the rung with one hand and reaches his grimy fingers toward my poor, defenseless armpit.

Okay. I'm not gonna lie, I'm *extremely* ticklish. As in laugh-like-a-little-girl ticklish. I can't help it! And that's *all* I need, to laugh like a preschool girl in front of just about everyone.

I would have to move away from Oak Glen *forever*. Maybe to some foreign land.

You can do this, I tell myself as Jared's horrible fingers are almost touching me. Just hang in there, dude. Just—

BRI-I-I-N-N-N-G! goes the buzzer.

And I, EllRay Jakes, have officially been saved by the bell.

I have *completed my challenge*.

I drop to the sand with a *thunk* and just lie there, trying to remember how to move. I see some legs walking up to me. "I guess you did it, dog," Kevin's voice says.

I think I almost hear some admiration in his words!

And then he's gone.

"C'mon, EllRay," Emma urges. "We gotta get to class." She sounds both confused and worried.

I guess boys are a mystery to her.

It's because we do stuff for different reasons than girls do, that's the thing.

Our reasons are good. Theirs are random.

"Yeah. C'mon," Corey says. And he hauls me to my feet.

Corey is abnormally strong, even though he's a skinny guy. It's probably because of all that swimming. His muscles are hiding out, but they're *there*.

"You gotta walk, EllRay," he tells me. "Left, right. Left, right. Move!"

"How long was I hanging there?" I ask as I scuffle my too-heavy feet through the sand, my sore arms hanging down like logs.

My hands are *killing* me. Each one feels as big as a bunch of bananas.

Hot bananas.

And I've got blisters! They're popping up like grapes.

"I dunno," Corey says. "A couple of minutes, maybe?"

"It had to be ten minutes, *easy*," I argue with as much strength as I can pull together. "Maybe even fifteen."

"Whatever you say, dog," Corey says. But I can tell he's just humoring me.

Who cares, though?

I did it!

✳ 13 ✳

THURSDAY'S CHALLENGE

"What's with all the blisters, buddy?" Dad asks me at dinner Wednesday night, reaching over to examine my hands. "Your mom mentioned you were hurting."

"I'm okay," I tell him. "We were just playing. You know, grabbing stuff."

"It looks like you've been out chopping down Christmas trees," he jokes. "Which reminds me," he adds, raising a finger. "I thought it might be fun for us to harvest our own tree this weekend, after the assembly—EllRay's big day—is behind us."

"It's not my big day," I object. "And you're not coming, are you? You just went to the P.T.A. meeting. Don't you have to work?"

"Of course I'll be there," Dad says. "I moved some appointments around. I don't want to miss seeing you do us proud, son."

Do us proud.

Does he mean *our-family*-us, or *the-community*-us?

I can't ask. But either way, **YOW**.

Too much pressure.

"What do you mean, 'harvest our own twee'?" Alfie asks, frowning.

"You know," Dad explains. "Saw it down ourselves. There's a Christmas tree farm not too far out of town. There was a feature in the local paper about it."

"That sounds like fun," Mom says. She likes having a real, live—well, dead—Christmas tree in the house each year. "I could pack a picnic," she adds. "And we can take some pictures."

Events are very well photographed in our family, thanks to my mom. First time crawling, first steps, first days of school, birthdays, new clothes. Special assemblies, for sure. You name it, and Mom's been there with a camera.

Alfie's fork droops. "Saw it down?" she asks, sounding like Dad has just suggested going out and strangling a turkey for our holiday dinner. "Instead of buying it at the Christmas twee store?"

"But Alfie," I say, trying to reason with her. "Where do you think all the trees in the Christmas tree stores come from? Christmas tree farms, that's where. People make their living growing them. So it's the same thing, really."

"No. They come from the North Pole," Alfie says, like she's answering an especially lame riddle. "*Weally*," she adds, determined to have the last word.

Mom, Dad, and I exchange quick, secret looks, trying silently to figure out what to say next to avoid one of her meltdowns. "Well, moving on," Mom finally says. "Who wants some dessert? We have applesauce or ice cream."

Guess which one I choose?

It is now Thursday morning, the day before the big assembly, *An Oak Glen Winter Wonderland*. But I have a feeling that *today* is going to be a big day, too—because I'm pretty sure Kevin's going to come up with a Thursday challenge for me.

What's it gonna be?

It's raining out, *hard*, so at least my poor hands will get off easy this time.

"Let's go through our song, girls and boys," Ms. Sanchez says after taking attendance. Each class has just started practicing its song, so there won't be time for a big group rehearsal. But since I will be the emcee for the first assembly, I know what the songs will be. Ms. Sanchez gave me a list so I could learn how to announce them.

1. The kindergarteners will sing "Jingle Bells," complete with construction paper antlers tied around their heads—though I'm not sure why they always pretend to be reindeer. Because it's tradition, I guess.

2. The first grade is singing "Frosty the Snowman." No drama there.

3. Second grade will sing "You're a Mean One, Mr. Grinch," which should be funny. I wish we'd gotten that song!

4. And we third-graders are singing "Jingle Bell Rock," like we planned, only we're singing the whole thing twice. The girls will do their jingle bell dance in the middle of it. Seeing their moves,

Ms. Sanchez has already warned them to "tone it down a little." But judging from their rehearsals at recess, anything could happen.

So, perfect! There's nothing about religion—or sugar—in any of the songs, which I guess will make Principal James and any grouchy parents happy.

Ms. Sanchez says the words to a song are called "lyrics." "Jingle Bell Rock" has some weird lyrics, no offense. I've heard the song before and one of the first lines says, "Blowing up bushels of fun." I'm not even kidding! I'm surprised we're allowed to sing about blowing things up, much less at Christmastime. I mean, at Winter Wonderland time. But us boys will probably sing that line the loudest.

KA-BLAMMM-O!

"EllRay. Listen up," Kevin whispers as Fiona McNulty passes out the lyrics—which we are supposed to have memorized by tomorrow, *ha, ha*. "Challenge number two, dude. You have to say 'I love you' to Fiona when she hands you the paper."

"*What*?" I say, trying not to squawk. "Dude. This is really challenge number three, counting the emcee thing."

"And you have to say it so she can hear you," Kevin adds, ignoring my argument. *"No whispering."*

A couple of guys—Jared and Stanley, anyway—must have been given the heads-up on this second challenge, because they're grinning big-time, watching and waiting.

So, I guess they're in on what's happening, now.

And Fiona and her weak ankles are getting closer.

Look. I like Fiona McNulty just fine, especially when we're doing art. You get good ideas just from spying on what she does. But *Kevin's* the one who kind of likes her. So this is just weird!

And now, she is nearing my desk.

And I have to say I love her.

Only doing this, and then completing the final challenge, using Kevin's messed-up arithmetic, will balance things out between me and him.

And then we can be friends, and everything will blend together again.

She's getting closer.

Closer.

Closer.

She hands one of the papers to Emma, who sits

next to me. Fiona is acting important, I notice—
as if she has been appointed Ms. Sanchez's official
Vice Teacher. Maybe permanently.

"Here you go, EllRay," she says, handing me a
piece of paper.

I guess the jingle hop *has* begun.

"Thanks, Fiona," I say. "I love you. Have a nice
day," I add, all in the exact same tone of voice.

Fiona, who is already handing the lyrics to Kry
Rodriguez, stops.

She just *stops*.

And then she backs up a few steps, as if she has thrown herself into reverse. *BEEP! BEEP! BEEP!*

"*What* did you just say to me?" she asks. It's like my words just gave her an electric shock.

Well, she's not the only one. I can't even feel my face.

"I said, 'Thanks, Fiona,'" I tell her, studying the words to the song. *Supposedly.*

"I mean after that," Fiona says.

"After that, what?" I ask, looking up at her and blinking, to show how innocent I am.

Hey. I said it once. No one said anything about saying it *twice.*

"What did you say after that?" she asks.

"I said, 'Have a nice day,'" I tell Fiona.

She narrows her eyes. "You'd better not be making fun of me, EllRay Jakes, or you're gonna get it," she whispers.

Right. What's she going to do? Crayon all over me with feathery strokes until I apologize?

But I have to admit, she looks like she's on the edge of hurt feelings. "I'm not making fun," I tell her quietly.

And that's the solid truth. I'm not.

I'm just trying to complete this challenge.

"Fiona! Finish up, *if you please*, so we can all start singing," Ms. Sanchez calls out. And Fiona shoots me one last look.

I sneak a glance at Kevin, who is shaking with silent laughter. He gives me a thumbs-up, though.

He would be high-fiving Jared and Stanley, if he could.

But who cares? I completed the second— *third!*—challenge.

✳ 14 ✳

PAYING CLOSE ATTENTION

"EllRay," Ms. Sanchez says at two-thirty, just after recess. "Can you stay after school for just a bit?"

It is an hour before class lets out for the day, and we are each working on a Personal Timeline, even though tomorrow is the last day of school before Christmas vacation. I mean before Winter Wonderland vacation. But I guess Ms. Sanchez is determined to get some schoolwork done today.

A timeline is a graph that uses a line to show the passage of time. We get to make any kind of timeline we want, which is pretty cool. I am making a timeline of the third grade so far, from September to now. Emma McGraw wants to be a nature scientist someday, so she is making a timeline showing the life of a typical mouse. Spoiler alert: it does not have a happy ending.

Corey Robinson—the champion swimmer—

is making a timeline that will start when he first learned to dog-paddle. It will probably end in the future, at the Olympics. And Cynthia Harbison is doing a timeline she is calling "Cynthia Harbison's History of the Universe," only I don't think she'll finish in time to hand it in.

"I thought you and I might run through what you're going to say at the assembly tomorrow morning," Ms. Sanchez says.

"Sure. But can you call my mom and ask her to pick me up late?" I ask.

See, Mom's driving me home today because of the rain. But I know she won't mind picking me up later than usual, She and Alfie will probably go out for hot chocolate at Grounds for Fun, Mom's favorite place to hang with other writers. "Can you please tell her that I want hot chocolate, if she gets any? With whipped cream on top?" I ask.

"Will do," Ms. Sanchez says, making an invisible check mark in the air. "And I'll give her my order as well," she adds, joking.

"Mom would get something for you," I tell her. "Really. She'd be happy to."

"I know she would, sweetie," Ms. Sanchez says,

laughing. "She's a peach. I guess it runs in the family."

"Huh," I say, trying to figure out whether or not that is a compliment.

But I decide to decide that it is.

I think that's the best way to handle comments like that, when you're not sure.

"Okay," Ms. Sanchez says after the last kid has shuffled out the door. "Only one more day to go, Mr. Jakes, and then we're *off*. For seventeen whole days!"

"Huh," I say again, even though Dad doesn't like me to say "huh" at home. I'm supposed to say, "Oh," I guess. Only I don't really get the difference. They're both just sounds.

But—Ms. Sanchez seems so happy about school letting out! I mean, *I'm* glad that school's going to be over for so long. But I didn't think a teacher would be happy about it. Not *our* teacher.

We're not that bad, are we? Us kids?

Won't she miss us, at least a little?

"Listen, EllRay," Ms. Sanchez begins. "Our assembly is going to start at around nine-thirty tomorrow morning, so right after attendance, we'll do one last run-through of the song, and then begin our calm, orderly trek to the auditorium."

"Okay," I say, even though I think she was being sarcastic with that last part.

"Then we'll probably all say the Pledge of Allegiance," she says. "And Principal James will welcome everyone to Oak Glen Primary School. Then he'll introduce *you*, the emcee."

"Okay," I say again, starting to feel kind of hot and tingly.

I am really going to have to do this.

"So, what were you planning to say?" Ms. Sanchez asks, tilting her head. The shiny black hair in her bun is falling down a little, the way it does at the end of the day, and her brown eyes look tired. But she is paying close attention to me.

"I was gonna say 'Hi,'" I tell her. "And then I was gonna say, 'Here are the kindergarten kids, singing something just for you.' And, like, do that for all the grades."

Ms. Sanchez thinks for a few seconds. "Maybe a

little more preparation might not be a bad thing," she finally suggests.

That means more preparation would be a *good* thing. Grownups sometimes say things backward. You have to learn to translate.

"How much preparation?" I ask. Because I'm no good at memorizing things—especially stuff I'm going to have to say in front of a zillion people. Including strangers.

"Just a little," she assures me. "For instance, you need a nice, short opening, and a good strong closing so people will know *An Oak Glen Winter Wonderland* is really and truly over, and they can go home. And, as you said, there should be a brief introduction for the song each of the four grades will perform."

Ms. Sanchez really wants me to do a good job. I can tell!

This makes me feel happy and nervous at the same time.

"I don't have to tell any jokes, do I?" I say.

"Heavens, no," Ms. Sanchez says, shaking her head. "Just, 'Hello, and welcome to *An Oak Glen Winter Wonderland*. Right into the mic, and

speak *slowly*. Because rushing through the words is the number-one mistake most people make when speaking to a crowd. Now, you give it a try."

"*Hello-o-o!*" I say, my voice sounding robot-slow as I form the first word. "Welcome to a Winter Wonderland. In Oak Glen," I finish. And then I wonder where I went wrong. It seemed so easy when she said it.

"Welcome to *An Oak Glen Winter Wonderland*," Ms. Sanchez tells me again.

"Okay. I got it. 'Hello," I say, shouting the word. "And welcome to a Winter Wonderland! At Oak Glen Primary School! No, wait."

"That would work just fine, EllRay," Ms. Sanchez says, smiling. "That's basically right."

"But I want to be *exactly* right," I tell her. "My dad's gonna be there! And my mom. And Alfie," I add.

I think Ms. Sanchez gets it about my dad. "Well, if you want to memorize the first part exactly," she says, "just remember that O comes before W in the alphabet. See? 'Oak Glen' comes before 'Winter Wonderland.'"

"Hello, Oak Glen! And welcome to a Winter Wonderland," I **SHOUT** again—a moment before stomping my foot. "Dang!" I say, scolding myself.

"But see, that was just fine, too," Ms. Sanchez tells me. "And then if you add a nice, loud 'Thanks for coming!' at the end of our song, you'll be home free. It's not like you have to be word perfect."

Hey. Is she giving up on me already?

"I don't even get why he chose me, anyway," I mumble. "Or why *you* chose me,' I add, my voice getting stronger. "I mean, why you chose me and Kevin to take the envelope to Principal James's office. You could have chosen anyone! A girl would have begged to take it. She would have been *honored*."

Emma. Annie Pat. Fiona. Kry. Cynthia.

Ms. Sanchez looks up, as if the answer might be written on the ceiling. "I can't honestly remember why I chose you that day," she finally says.

And I believe her. I really do.

✳ **15** ✳

BEING SINGLED OUT

I take a deep breath before speaking again. "But you do know why the principal wanted Kevin or me to be the emcee, don't you?" I say, daring to look her in the eye.

"I'm not sure—" she begins, protesting.

"It's because we have brown skin, right?" I say, interrupting Ms. Sanchez for the first time in my life. "I mean, I think the *principal's* the one who came up with the idea of maybe calling the assembly Diversity Day," I add, my heart pounding. "You know, at the P.T.A. meeting. My dad told me. And me and Kevin are just about the only diversity the principal's got. In the third grade, anyway."

"It just happened to work out that way this year," Ms. Sanchez says, shaking her head. "But maybe skin color *was* on his mind when he chose you," she tells me. "I don't know, EllRay. I honestly don't think it was, but I can't speak for Principal James. You could always ask him. But would it be such a bad thing if it was true? Principal James wants more diversity at Oak Glen. And he knows you'll do a fine job. So why *not* you?"

"You don't know what it's like," I say, looking away.

"I don't know what it's like?" she asks. "EllRay, please, I, Yvette Carolina Angela Sanchez Verdugo, don't know what it's like being singled out because of the color of my skin?"

OOPS. Big-time. "Verdugo?" I ask, just for something to say.

"Verdugo was my mother's maiden name," she explains. "And that's the traditional way to say it. But I go by Sanchez, to make things easier for people."

"Oh. But you're barely even brown," I say, trying too late to defend myself.

"And you're not as brown as Kevin," Ms. Sanchez says. "And Kevin's not as brown as Mrs. Jenkins in the office. It's not a contest, EllRay."

"Did kids used to pick on you when you were little?" I ask, afraid of what her answer might be.

Because we all really like Ms. Sanchez. Who would ever have wanted to be mean to her?

They wouldn't dare!

Ms. Sanchez frowns, scaring me for a second. "Are kids picking on *you*, EllRay? Because of your skin color, I mean?"

"No," I say. "If they yell at me, it's for other reasons. Like, maybe I get on someone's nerves. Or I hog the kickball. Or I step on their foot."

Or I hurt their feelings in front of other kids.

"Well, they'd better not *not* pick on you," she says, looking kind of fierce for the prettiest teacher at Oak Glen Primary School.

"But they picked on *you*?" I ask again.

And she nods. "I was born in the nineteen eighties, EllRay, and things had changed for the better by then, at least a little. But there were still plenty of bad times," she tells me. "I think things are better now, though. Not perfect, but better."

"That's good, I guess," I mumble.

"So, yes, children did pick on me," Ms. Sanchez says, a faraway look in her eyes. "*Un poquito*. A little. My older brothers came in for more of it, I'm sure. But there were a couple of bad names kids still used, even then," she tells me. "And once, an adult told me to go back where I came from."

"Why? Where did you come from?" I ask, curious. San Diego? Pasadena? *Cucamonga?*

Ms. Sanchez laughs. "Well, Los Angeles, as it happens. In fact, my mother's side of the family were landowners here in California long before it was even a state," she says. "Only she brought us up never to boast. Not that the man trying to insult me would have known anything about Old California history, or *Los Californianos.*"

"I hate him," I tell her.

"You don't have to hate people like that, sweetie," Ms. Sanchez says, smiling. "Just hate what they say. And feel sorry about those empty minds they have to lug around all day long."

"But—you're getting married next summer," I remind her. "And then you won't even *be* Ms. Sanchez anymore. You'll be Mrs. Timberlake, only not the famous one."

"He's famous with me, EllRay," she says, laughing. "And I'll still have brown skin. But in my heart,

I will always be Yvette Carolina Angela Sanchez Verdugo. And proud, too, no matter how modest and polite my mama was. And I'd be just as proud if my family had come here much more recently, by the way."

"Your skin's more caramel than brown," I say, trying to think how Fiona the artist would describe it in official crayon colors.

And I'm also thinking that *my* name, *Lancelot Raymond Jakes*, may be weird, or even the "EllRay" part, but at least it's not long. *That* long, anyway. It would take forever to write it! "Wait a minute. I'm almost finished," I picture Ms. Sanchez saying, whenever she has to write her name.

"My skin color is brown, EllRay. Just like yours," Ms. Sanchez insists.

"I guess it is," I say. And a warm, happy, *proud* feeling spreads through my chest.

Maybe Principal James did choose me to emcee for some complicated grownup reason of his own, or maybe it was pure accident. But I'll do a good job anyway.

"And you, young man, are going to do a fine job

at the assembly tomorrow morning," Ms. Sanchez says, reading my mind as usual. "Listen," she adds, inspired. "I have a special marker we can use. First thing tomorrow morning, I'll print the four songs you have to announce on the palm of your hand."

"But what about the introduction?" I ask. "Hello to a Winter Wonderland Welcome in Oak Glen, California," I say, trying again.

"That would work just fine," Ms. Sanchez tells me. "But I'll write down the correct sentence now, so you can practice it tonight. If you want to."

She prints fast, then glances up at the wall clock. "Oops," she says, surprised. "Your mom will be waiting for you, sweetie. Tell her I'm sorry I kept you so long, okay?"

"Okay," I say.

But *I'm* not sorry.

Not even one little bit.

✳ 16 ✳

LAST CHALLENGE

"We're supposed to wear red today," I yell into Mom and Dad's bedroom about five seconds after I wake up on Friday morning. "I forgot to tell you."

"Way-y-y ahead of you, EllRay," Mom says, coming out of her room. She is holding a newly-ironed red sweatshirt as if it is a masterpiece she just finished painting.

And who—besides my mom—irons a sweatshirt?

That's how important today is to her. And to Dad. And maybe even to Alfie.

"Red enough for you?" Mom jokes. "Listen," she adds, seeing my surprise. "I'm the room parent, remember. I'm the one who sent out the e-mail last week about wearing a red top, if possible."

Alfie stumbles out of her bedroom, rubbing her eyes. "Where's mine?" she asks Mom.

"Still on the ironing board," Mom says.

"You mean we're gonna be dressed alike?" I say, but Mom just laughs.

"You *know* Miss Alfie would never wear a plain old sweatshirt," she tells me, shaking her head. "Hers has a beautiful brown angel on the front, with lacy white wings that stick out a little. It's adorable."

Alfie beams. "My angel's got a sparkly halo, too," she tells me. "If Santa Claus *is* spying on me, he'll think I look cute. And *good*, EllWay, because of the halo. So no tattling."

"Nervous?" Mom asks me, draping the red sweatshirt over my arm with care. "Did you get a good night's sleep?"

"I got a *bad* night's sleep," I inform her. And it's true, because I had weird dreams all night long. I don't remember them, but I could use a nap. And I haven't even had breakfast yet.

"Well, let me finish up with Alfie's outfit, then I'll scramble some eggs. You need some protein in that tummy," Mom tells me.

I'm afraid that if I put *anything* in "that tummy," as Mom called it, there's gonna be a tummy-related disaster. Maybe all over the Oak Glen Primary School stage.

BLAR-R-R-R-T!

But I'm too tired to argue with her, so I keep my mouth shut.

"All right, everyone," Ms. Sanchez calls out, clapping her hands to get our attention after the last in-class rehearsal. "It's time to walk to the auditorium. *Quietly*," she adds, raising a warning finger. "Muffle your jingle bells, ladies."

And the girls clasp their bells to their chests so they won't give away our class's noisy surprise.

We are feeling excited for three reasons. First, today is different from other school days. Second, we are about to perform onstage, in front of a lot of strangers. And third, winter break is about to start. And you can add a fourth excitement for me, because I'm the emcee.

As she promised, Ms. Sanchez used a special pen to print short versions of the four acts on one of my palms.

1. K: Jingle Bells.
2. First: Frosty.
3. Second: Mean Grinch.
4. Third: Jingle Bell Rock.

And on my other palm, she printed, very small, "Welcome to Wonderland!" and "Thanks for coming!" This is followed by "NICE AND SLOW."

Now, all I have to do is to *not sweat*, because I want to be able to read her writing. And because *I want to do a good job.*

I really do! I know that now.

1. I want to do a good job for Oak Glen Primary School.
2. And I want to do a good job for Ms. Sanchez, and for our bright-red third grade class.
3. And I want to do a good job for my mom and dad and little sister.
4. I even want to do a good job for the community, as Dad calls it. Not that the community will notice.
5. But I especially want to do a good job for myself.

Maybe I *am* a natural leader! Who knows? But if I am, I have to start someplace.

Who cares what Principal Hairy James's reason was when he said that either Kevin or I had to be the emcee? And who cares why Kevin told me I should do it?

None of that matters anymore.

"Dude, listen," Kevin McKinley whispers as we work our way down the main hall, which is still decorated with those Frisbee-sized snowflakes.

"What?" I say, interrupting my silent practice.

"I figured out your last challenge," he says. He has a funny look on his face, like he wants to apologize ahead of time for something.

"I already did three," I remind him.

"Tell him," Jared urges in his version of a quiet voice.

"Yeah. Tell him," Stanley says, grinning like a hyena.

Oh. So that's how it is. Jared and Stanley are running things, now!

A couple of girls are looking at us as we whisper and walk, but we ignore them.

"Okay," Kevin says, his voice shaking a little. "At the end of the show, right after you say, 'Thanks for coming,' you have to yell out a swear."

"A good one, too," Jared says.

He means a *bad* one. A bad swear word.

I'm doomed.

If I *do it*, I'm doomed.

This challenge is definitely coming from Jared, and maybe from Stanley, too. Not Kevin. And it's more of a dare than a challenge, if you ask me. Because this is not something I would ever want to do.

Anyway, my deal was with Kevin.

And doing a dare was not part of that deal.

Jared pokes Kevin in the back to make him speak, like Kevin is a ventriloquist's dummy. "You have to yell it real loud, and in front of everyone," Kevin whispers, right on cue. In case I didn't get it.

But I got it.

Kevin looks miserable, though.

"Listen," I whisper back, trying to talk only to him. "It'll wreck the whole show."

"Who cares?" Jared says, butting in. "You're not so great, *EllRay*. Just because you get to be the emcee."

He sounds jealous! And he would just *love* to see me get in trouble.

"I know I'm not so great," I tell him—and Stanley, and Kevin. "But the class *practiced*," I remind them. "And the girls are really excited about dancing. And Ms. Sanchez got all dressed up. And our parents are gonna be there."

"Not *my* parents," Jared says.

Oh, right.

They almost never come to anything.

Jared and Stanley are messing with Kevin *and* me. Not only me. But how do I get Kevin to see that?

And they're doing it because they think they can. No other reason.

I need to stop the clock, I think, my heart thunking as we plod down the hall.

I need time to figure out all the reasons why this is so wrong, in so many ways.

And I need time to explain everything to Kevin, including how sorry I am about what happened, and how cool it was being friends with him.

But also about why I'm not gonna yell out the swear, even if it means having no friends at all except Corey.

I mean, I'm not *perfect*. It's not like I wouldn't do something goofy and random! But it would have to be my own idea. And not hurt anyone else. And it wouldn't be *this*.

Only I can't stop time, because I am not a *Die, Creature, Die* superhero.

And we're almost at the auditorium.

The show is about to start.

"They made me do this," Kevin whispers again, speaking so only I can hear. "But just say the swear, so they'll still like me. And then you and I can be friends again."

I try to look him in the eye. "But listen, I can't—"

"But nothin'," Stanley says, giving me a shove.

And I think, for one crazy second, of telling *Stanley* about my dad's "Mr. G," and how Stanley should have stuck a G at the end of "nothing," since we supposedly paid for all twenty-six letters of the alphabet.

But I don't.

I may be doomed, but I'm not *nuts*!

And anyway, Mr. G is Dad's thing.

Not mine.

✳ **17** ✳

AN OAK GLEN WINTER WONDERLAND

It is almost time for me to introduce the third grade class. I feel sick to my stomach, knowing the terrible thing that I am supposed to do, only I won't.

I am sitting on a folding chair backstage next to Miss Myrna, the lady who organizes things that happen in the auditorium. She suspects nothing.

The kindergartners were cute singing "Jingle Bells." The first-graders did okay singing "Frosty the Snowman," except before they started, one little guy was so scared that he refused to go onstage. So I let him sit and cry on my folding chair until his class's song was done. And then he ran onstage to take a huge old bow.

It was like he'd been the star of the show!

Now the striped-muffler-wearing second-graders are finishing their song, "You're a Mean One, Mr.

Grinch." The whole audience is laughing, because Mr. Havens—the second grade teacher—is onstage wearing a Mr. Grinch costume. And the littlest girl in their class is dressed up as Cindy Lou Who. They even got her hair right.

The lyrics to that song are really hard, so the second-graders get to hold them while they sing. But during the entire song, Mr. Havens has been creeping around, pretending to scare kids or steal their mufflers or grab their music, while tiny Cindy Lou Who skitters after him.

"Aww," Miss Myrna coos, clasping her hands as she watches Cindy Lou Who skip across the stage.

This will be a hard act for us third-graders to follow! And *An Oak Glen Winter Wonderland* is already running twelve minutes late. Getting all the kids out of their auditorium seats, up onto the stage, and then back into their seats is what has chewed up the time.

In the front row, Principal James keeps looking at his watch.

You think you have problems *now*, Principal James? What if I was about to break every law in the school system—and maybe the universe—by shouting out a swear at the very end of the show?

It would be like a meteor crashing through the atmosphere to Earth right here in Oak Glen, California! And becoming a meteorite. Remember?

Only I will never get credit for *not doing* something. Which is not fair.

Maybe I *should* do it? My friend problems would be over if I did.

But my grownup problems would be just beginning.

Also my me problems. They count, too.

Because shouting out the swear would just be *wrong*.

Poor Kevin, I think, feeling sorry for him in advance. I mean, he got me into all this. But when I don't yell out the swear, Jared and Stanley won't be friends with him anymore. For a while, at least. It will blow over, though.

But—I already did three challenges, right? And I *told* Kevin no dares!

Anyway, Kevin didn't even come up with this one. It was Jared and Stanley all the way.

Oops. The pre-recorded "Grinch" music is finishing up, even though each kid seems to be singing a different line. But at least it's coming to an end.

And the audience **WHOOPS**, claps, and yells like crazy while the second-graders bow funny, fist pump, or curtsey, depending on the kid.

I peek out from behind the curtain and see Ms. Sanchez trying to get our class lined up in the aisle, so they'll be ready to sprint up to the stage after I announce the final song. The girls are tying the bell straps to their ankles as quietly as they can.

Which isn't very quietly.

Miss Myrna jabs me between my shoulder blades with a surprisingly sharp finger, which means it's time for me to do my emcee thing again. I get to my feet and stagger Frankenstein-like to the microphone standing in the middle of the stage.

Talk about not blending in!

"And now," I say into the mic, "I present to you Ms. Sanchez's awesome third grade class singing 'Jingle Bell Rock.' Come on up, third-graders!"

I'm supposed to join them after they're all on-stage, and then step forward when we're done, so I can tell the audience good-bye.

Time *finally* seems to switch into slow motion

as my classmates stomp and jangle their way up to the stage. Miss Myrna quickly wrangles the boys—including me—into a line in the back, and she herds the jingly girls to the front. Then she scurries backstage to start our music.

And some little Anza-Borrego earthquake fault splits open in my brain, and I see that this is just one of probably a million times in my life when I will have to make a decision like this.

And each decision I make will belong *only to me*, if I have anything to say about it. Which I will.

My decisions won't belong to my mom and dad. Not to Corey or Kevin, either. And for sure, not to Jared.

Also, some of those decisions—like this one, maybe?—will be very important.

But the weird thing is, I have a feeling that you can't always tell at the time how important a decision will be. You can only see it when you look back! So you gotta make each one *on purpose*.

And I have made the right decision.

I wriggle in next to Kevin, changing places with Corey. "Listen, Kev," I whisper to Kevin. "I want us to be friends again, but I'm not gonna yell out a swear. And you shouldn't have asked me to, because I already did three challenges."

Kevin gapes at me. "But EllRay. You have to do it, or else—"

"And this last one wasn't even your idea," I interrupt. "And—and *Alfie's wearing a brand-new angel sweatshirt*," I say, the words tumbling out of nowhere. "She was dancing in the aisle during the last song, dude! She thinks she's at a *rock concert*."

Kevin has a soft spot for Alfie. Don't ask me why.

"*Shhh*," a few girls say, half-turning to glare at us as we wait for the music to begin.

"I just wanted to give you a heads-up, Kev," I tell him. "Out of my complete and total respect for you."

But he just looks at me like all hope is lost.

Sorry, Kevin. It's been fun being friends with you, dog. And I was looking forward to teaching you *Die, Creature, Die*, so we could all play it together.

Our music starts.

✳ **18** ✳

A NOT-SO-PERFECT CHRISTMAS

"Hey, buddy," Dad says, poking his head into my room at ten-thirty p.m. on Christmas Eve. "Too excited to sleep? I can hear the wheels turning in here."

This means he can supposedly hear me thinking. Of course he can't, but it's true that my brain is buzzing. Today has been packed so full that I am numb.

And it's true, I cannot fall asleep.

It rained all day, but that didn't slow us down much—though Alfie worried aloud about Santa's reindeer slipping tonight on our wet tile roof. Dad didn't calm her down any when he joked that Santa might sue us if he fell.

"Don't say that, Dad," she said. "He might be *wistening*."

Which is Alfie-speak for listening.

"I guess I'm excited about Christmas," I tell my dad. "But I also feel kind of—"

"Sad? Nervous?" Dad says, trying out a couple of sentence endings for me.

I nod my head the best that I can on my pillow.

It's hard to explain my mixed-up feelings. But my dad seems to understand.

"I remember that feeling," Dad says. "You're nervous that maybe you won't get what you want tomorrow. Or even if you do, you're sad in advance because Christmas morning will be over so fast."

"And I'm *not* sure about what I got for Mom," I tell him. "That napkin holder with the chickens painted on it, remember? I don't think it's good enough."

"Listen, son," my dad says, sitting on the edge of my bed. "Nothing is good enough for your mom, because she's the absolute best. She's our queen. But she's going to love it. It will go right on the kitchen table, just you wait and see."

"She would pretend, though," I say. "I want her to *really* like it."

"Well, you have no control over that, EllRay,"

Dad says, laughing. "None of us does. But that's Christmas for you! Maybe all we can do is to try hard, and then *hope* for the best. Did I ever tell you about my most perfect Christmas ever? The year I got exactly what I wanted, and then some?"

"Nuh-uh," I say, shaking my head in the dark as Dad settles in next to me, on top of the covers.

I love my dad's stories about when he was a kid.

"It must have been, oh, when I was nine years old, just a year older than you are now. And the biggest 'wow' toy that Christmas was the Nintendo Entertainment System." He sighs, remembering. "It was really expensive," he says. "Something like one hundred and fifty dollars, which was a *lot* back then. And the games were forty or fifty dollars each. I don't know."

"That's a lot even today," I point out. "I mean, *really* a lot."

"True," Dad says, nodding in the dark. "And you know Pop-Pop," he says, talking about my grandfather, who lives near San Francisco now. "He was always careful with a dollar, so I was *sure* he and Mama weren't going to get it for me. And even now, people call that Nintendo the single greatest video game console in history," Dad adds, sounding like the hopeful nine-year-old kid he was back then. "That's how good it was."

"But Pop-Pop was a doctor," I say. "Don't doctors make a lot of money?"

"Some do," Dad agrees. "But Pop-Pop was just starting out back then, and he was not in private practice. He was a *Navy* doctor. You know, at the Naval Hospital San Diego? It became the Medical Center a short while later," he adds.

But I want Dad to stick with his perfect Christmas story.

"I guess you got it, though," I say, prodding him to tell me what happened.

"Not only did I get it," Dad says, "but I also got the G.I. Joes that were on my list. Mercer, Red, Dog, and Taurus," he says, still sounding impressed all these years later. "And on top of everything else, my grandparents gave me this really special toy called Talking Alf. 'A.L.F.' stood for 'Alien Life Form.' It was a hit TV series, see, and I just loved it. And Talking Alf was really expensive too. But oh, how I wanted that toy—because sometimes, I think I felt like an alien, too."

My own dad felt like he didn't blend in? Was it because he had brown skin?

Well, he still does.

I *do not* like talking to my dad about skin color, he is so prickly about it. But I also want to, at least a little. "Why?" I ask, my heart pounding. "Didn't you have a very big community, either? Is that why you felt like an alien? Not that I'm complaining," I add quickly.

"It was a much bigger community than ours is now, son," Dad tells me, laughing and shaking his head at the same time. I can feel it in the dark. "Even if the African-American population was pretty small in San Diego back then. Some gang action had Pop-Pop pretty concerned, though. But no," he continues. "I think I identified with Alf because my interests were so different from those of my friends. Good old science," he explains, shrugging.

"But what did Talking Alf do that was so great?" I ask, trying to understand.

"He had a cassette player inside him, and you'd put a cassette in, and his mouth would move as he told you stories about outer space," Dad says.

"It was the latest cool thing, and I thought I could learn something from him."

"What's a cassette tape?" I ask, and Dad shakes his head again in the dark. "It's kind of what CDs used to be. But never mind," he says, like it's too hard to explain. "The point is, for the first time in my life, I got everything I'd even dreamed of getting."

"And you were *so happy*," I say, finishing his story for him.

I'm smiling **BIG** in the dark.

"I was," Dad agrees. "For about half an hour. And then, guess what?"

"What?" I ask, my eyes wide. "You woke up, and it was all a dream?"

"No. It was real, all right," Dad says. "But I started worrying. What about the next year? And the year after that? Could Christmas ever be that perfect again?"

Now *I'm* the one who is shaking his head, picturing my worrywart nine-year-old father freaking out about his probably-not-perfect future. Who would've guessed?

"And you know what?" he asks, laughing. "I was right! Christmas never *was* that good again when I was a kid. But it turns out that's okay. Each one was still fun, and I survived."

"But—does that mean nothing's ever perfect forever, or even *easy*, from start to finish?" I ask Dad. "Not even something built-in good, like Christmas?"

It sounds strange, but this is giving me an idea!

"It's okay, though," Dad says again. "That's my point."

"Then listen," I tell him, excited. "Maybe we should always just go ahead and mess up some of the small stuff. You know, get it over with! And we've already done that this year—like when we brought home that crooked Charlie Brown Christmas tree Alfie felt sorry for. Or when you sat down on the box of ornaments after dinner tonight. Or when Alfie found out she accidentally put her *Fuzzy Kitties* DVD in the *Elf* box, and now *Elf* is lost forever."

"Lost in the black hole that is Miss Alfie's room," Dad says, laughing. "And only the ghost of Talking Alf knows where it is, but he's not saying. You may be onto something, son."

"And then we could just give up early on Christmas being perfect, and *relax*," I say, finishing my thought. "We can have a not-so-perfect Christmas!"

"Now, that is some pretty cool thinking," Dad says. "But there might still be a few mixed feelings about the holiday."

"Yeah, but we'd *expect* them," I explain. "We'd say, 'Man, this is *messed up*, just like I thought it would be. Typical Christmas!' And it would be *funny*."

"Well, I know one thing for sure," Dad says, sounding happy in the dark. "You and I are going camping in Anza-Borrego on the twenty-eighth, come what may. That's just four more days. Our reservations are all set, buddy. And maybe this trip will give us a chance to find our feet again."

Hmm, I think, **WRIGGLING** my toes. I already know where *my* feet are.

But I kind of understand what he means. "You used to camp there with Pop-Pop, didn't you?" I ask. "When you were a kid?"

"Nearly every year, if we were lucky with the weather," Dad says.

"You and I should mess things up ahead of time. On purpose, Dad," I say, putting my new theory into action. "Just a little. You know, forget a ground cloth, or lose the marshmallows for the s'mores.

Nothing huge," I say. "Just enough so that it takes the pressure off us trying to have a perfect trip."

"EllRay, you're too much," Dad says, reaching over in the dark to knuckle-rub my head, which, like I said before, is his version of a hug. "Do you realize how proud of you your mom and I are? And how much we love you?"

Oh, great, I think, ducking my head away from him and scowling at the wall next to my bed. That dumb *assembly* again. "But I keep telling you guys," I say. "It was just an accident that I was the emcee. It wasn't because I was like a special representative of the community, or anything. That would be too much for me." I add, almost in a whisper.

It *would* be too much. For any kid.

"Well, you did a fine job, son," Dad says. "But I wasn't talking about the assembly *or* the community."

"What else are you proud of me for?" I ask, turning partway back to him.

"Oh, a dozen things," Dad says, laughing.

"Like what? Name three," I say, whispering those last words.

"I'll name five," Dad says, accepting the challenge. "Number one, I'm proud of what a good big brother you are to Alfie, even when she makes it difficult."

"Which she does, sometimes," I say.

"Number two, I'm proud of what a good son you are to Mom and me. You're easy to be around, and you do your chores without too much complaining. And you don't make excuses or blame other people when you do mess up."

"Huh," I say, pleased. And I'm thinking—Dad makes lists, just like I do? I guess it runs in the family!

"Number three, I'm proud of what a good friend you are," Dad continues. "And you pay attention to your friendships, too. You take care of them."

"I don't have *that* many friends," I tell Dad—just in case he's thinking I'm super-popular or something.

And, of course, I have to subtract Kevin. For now, at least.

That will change, though. Fingers crossed.

"But you have *good* friends," he says. "Number four, you work hard at school," Dad says. "Even when the going gets tough."

"And it can get pretty tough," I admit.

"And number five, I'm proud of the way you think, son. You have an original way of working things out for yourself that I really admire. Like tonight's 'Mess Up the Small Stuff' solution."

And that's not even half of it, I think, remembering how I decided not to shout out a swear at the assembly last Friday.

But there's such a thing as self-respect, isn't there? And not letting someone else try to get you in trouble?

I get to decide the **GOOFY** stuff I'm going to do! Or not do.

I'll decide when I'm going to blend in, and when I'm going to stand out.

"Are you asleep, buddy?" Dad asks in a barely-there voice.

"Almost," I tell him. "I think so, anyway."

"Then I'll say Merry Christmas, and good night," Dad says, getting to his feet and pulling the covers up over my shoulders. "See you in the not-so-perfect morning."

"Yeah. See you," I say, smiling as I roll over to go to sleep.

It's going to be a *very* Merry Christmas, no matter what, I think, wriggling down under my quilt.

A winter wonderland Christmas.

And if it isn't, well—there's always next year!

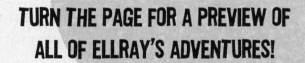

TURN THE PAGE FOR A PREVIEW OF
ALL OF ELLRAY'S ADVENTURES!

EllRay Jakes
is NOT a chicken!

EllRay Jakes may be the smallest kid in Ms. Sanchez's third-grade class, but he has a big personality! And he's not going to let Jared, the biggest kid in class, call him a chicken or get in the way of a trip to Disneyland. All EllRay has to do is stay out of trouble for one week—and keep away from Jared. The question is, can he do it?

EllRay Jakes
is a Rock Star!

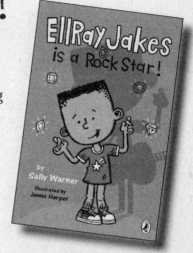

EllRay wishes he had something
cool to brag about. Everyone else
in his third-grade class does.
Jared's dad owns a brand-new
car with flames painted on it,
and Kevin's dad is rich, but all
EllRay's geologist dad has is a
collection of rocks. *Boring!* Or is it? They *are* from all
over the world . . . and when EllRay brings some of the
rocks into school, everyone is impressed. In fact, they're
so impressed, they keep them! Now EllRay needs a plan
to rescue his dad's rocks . . . before his big problem lands
him in *gigantic* trouble.

EllRay Jakes
walks the plank!

Things are going just swimmingly for EllRay. But everything comes screeching to a halt when his younger sister accidentally over-feeds the classroom goldfish EllRay was taking care of over spring vacation. Zippy is a goner. Fortunately, most of his classmates are sympathetic. But not bossy Cynthia. She sees this as an opportunity to blame EllRay for her own mess-ups. Must EllRay now walk the plank for stuff that he *didn't* do?

EllRay Jakes
the Dragon Slayer!

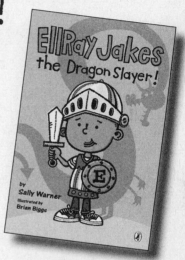

EllRay knows a thing or two about getting picked on. So when he sees his sister, Alfie, being bossed around by a dragon-like girl at her school, EllRay wants to share his wisdom. As her older (and wiser!) brother he has a duty to show her that she should stand up for herself. But it's a bit more complicated than he thought. Can EllRay help Alfie figure out her own way to slay this dragon?

EllRay Jakes
and the Beanstalk

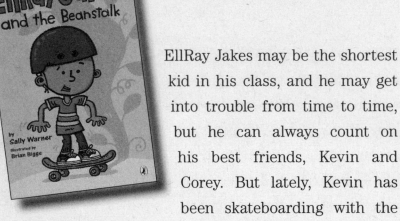

EllRay Jakes may be the shortest kid in his class, and he may get into trouble from time to time, but he can always count on his best friends, Kevin and Corey. But lately, Kevin has been skateboarding with the meanest boy in class. Could EllRay be losing one of his friends?

Not giving up without a fight, EllRay asks his older neighbor to show him a few jaw-dropping skateboard moves—like ollies and kickflips. EllRay must learn as many tricks as he can before the secret boys-only third-grade skate-off. But will it be enough?

EllRay Jakes is Magic!

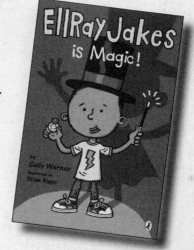

When EllRay and his friends hear about the school talent show, they're not impressed. They're too old for that stuff. But their teacher, Mrs. Sanchez, isn't so quick to let her students off the hook. Five students absolutely *must* try out, and EllRay somehow ends up being one of them. Now he has to figure out something he's talented at . . . like maybe magic?

But the pressure's on. It's up to EllRay to take the stage and show his classmates and the whole school that he's not only talented but *magic.*

EllRay Jakes
Rocks the Holidays!

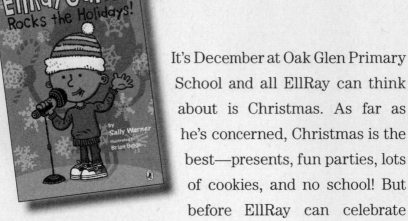

It's December at Oak Glen Primary School and all EllRay can think about is Christmas. As far as he's concerned, Christmas is the best—presents, fun parties, lots of cookies, and no school! But before EllRay can celebrate with his family, he must lead half the school (as the emcee) in the Winter Wonderland assembly.

How tough can it be to memorize a few lines? Very tough, especially when EllRay's soon-to-be ex-friend gives him a dare to perform onstage. If he completes the dare, he'll save his friendship . . . but he'll ruin the assembly. *And* get in enormous trouble.

EllRay is in for a not-so holly jolly time.